MOON SHOTS

Eight Vampire For Hire Stories

/ / / /

J.R. RAIN

SELECT BOOKS BY J.R. RAIN

VAMPIRE FOR HIRE
Moon Dance
Vampire Moon
American Vampire
Moon Child
Christmas Moon (novella)
Vampire Dawn
Vampire Games
Moon Island
Moon River
Vampire Sun
Moon Dragon
Moon Shadow
Vampire Fire
Midnight Moon
Moon Angel
Vampire Sire
Moon Master
Dead Moon
Lost Moon
Vampire Destiny
Infinite Moon (coming soon)

SAMANTHA MOON CASE FILES
Moon Bayou *(with Rod Kierkegaard)*
Blood Moon *(with Matthew S. Cox)*

Parallel Moon *(with Kris Carey)*

SAMANTHA MOON ORIGINS
with Matthew S. Cox
New Moon Rising
Moon Mourning
Haunted Moon

SAMANTHA MOON ADVENTURES
with Matthew S. Cox
Banshee Moon
Moon Monster
Moon Ripper
Witch Moon
Moon Goddess
Moon Blaze
Golem Moon
Moon Maidens

Published by
Crop Circle Books
212 Third Crater, Moon

Copyright © 2014 by J.R. Rain

All rights reserved.

Printed in the United States of America.

ISBN- 9798645317355

TABLE OF CONTENTS

Vampire Requiem   1.

Moon Love 37.

Moon Musings 98.

Moon Memories   125.

Moon Quiz 143.

Moon Beast   151.

Vampire Widow   197.

Moon Maze   209.

About the Author   255.

Vampire Requiem

Requiem: a song, chant or poem for someone who died.

"If death is the great equalizer, then some of us are just more equal than others."
—Diary of the Undead

She was the last person I ever thought I would be friends with.

Then again, when you've been through what we've been through together, well, maybe it's not so surprising, after all.

But still...

We sat together on the back steps of my house, facing my expansive back yard and the Pep Boys sign that hung like a god over the far wall.

Friends, of course, might be too strong a word. And *acquaintances* just didn't feel right, either. She was certainly no acquaintance, that was for sure. Not after some of the shit we'd shared.

A comrade, I thought. *A comrade-in-arms.*

Yeah, I liked the sound of that.

"Sounds, I dunno, a little Russian," Nancy said, picking up on my thoughts a little too quickly for my liking.

"Well, we're going with it," I said.

"Suit yourself," she said, shrugging, nonplussed. "And, for the love of God, will you blink?"

Admittedly, I didn't blink much when I was around her, since I knew it freaked her out. There was still some sass in me. Anyway, I could go for days without blinking. Generally, I had to remind myself to blink.

I now made a big show of blinking and she laughed and shook her head.

We were drinking wine and smoking cigarettes. One of us was buzzed and possibly laying the groundwork for lung cancer. The other would never get drunk or die of lung cancer, or die of anything other than silver to the heart. That someone, of course, just happened to be me. After a few minutes of silence, I asked, "How old are you?"

"Twenty-seven."

"You were..." I did the math "...twenty-two when you met him?"

"Something like that."

"You were old enough to know better," I

said.

She shrugged, some of her old defensiveness coming through. That she was a functioning human after what she had been through, was amazing. That she could acknowledge someone else's feelings was a surprise. After all, my dead husband's mistress had had a helluva childhood. I almost felt sorry for her. *Almost.*

She exhaled a long, billowing plume of blue-gray smoke and turned to me. "How old were you when you married Danny?"

"Twenty-one."

"Back when you were human?"

"I'm still human," I said, and might have snapped at her a little. "I'm just, you know, weird."

She laughed. "You are far more than weird."

I shrugged and smoked and wondered again how, of all people, she and I had become friends. Through Danny, of course, a man we had both slept with, shared life experiences with, and might have even loved. Well, I knew *I* had loved him. I couldn't vouch for her, although I *could* vouch for her if I scanned her thoughts. I didn't scan her thoughts. Truth was, I never wanted to scan her thoughts again. Her thoughts were dark and twisted—full of memories that no one should ever have. Also, the last thing I wanted to see was an image of

Danny in there, with her—and them going at it like feral rabbits.

"We never went at it like rabbits, Sam. Feral or otherwise."

"How much did Danny tell you about me?" I asked. I often wondered just how much he had blabbed. And were there others out there who knew my secret?

Other strippers and prostitutes, no doubt.

"I'm sure there are, Sam," she said, exhaling and looking away. Nancy never hid from what she did then and what she currently did now. Although I didn't ask, I got the very strong feeling—and these days I always trusted my feelings—that she made her living as a very high-priced call girl.

"Something like that, Sam. I could tell you about it if you really want to know."

"I don't want to know. Not now, not ever."

She shrugged and smoked and if my judgmental tone had affected her, she didn't show it. These days, I tried not to judge her. I tried to welcome her as a friend.

"I do what I have to do, Sam. I'm glad you don't judge me...too much. Anyway, he told me your whole story. How you were attacked. How you were turned. How you guys kept blood in the garage fridge. He told me more. Lots more. How you threatened him, scared him."

MOON SHOTS

Danny had blabbed my secret.

Months ago, when Nancy and I had first met, I could have denied it. I could have even changed her opinion of me. Controlling others was something that used to not sit well with me, but was now, admittedly, a feasible option. Of course, the demon bitch within me loved to control others. Loved it more than anything, if I had to guess. So, I rarely gave in to controlling others. And, yeah, that pissed her off to no end. Now, *that* I enjoyed.

"Are you taking his side?" I asked.

"Well, you did threaten him, Sam. He told me all about you throwing him down on the bed and choking—"

"He tried to have me killed! By other vampires. And he nearly got my sister killed, too."

She shrugged. She usually shrugged. It was her defense mechanism. Her shrugs seemed to indicate: *I've seen worse.*

I shielded my thoughts. I had to. They had turned dark. Far darker than I was willing to share.

"You're taking that rat bastard's side, aren't you? And if you shrug again, I'm going to remove your shoulder and feed it to my neighbor's dog."

She shrugged again, and this one was

defiant, snotty. It also came out with a surprising lack of concern for her own safety. She should have been very, very concerned for her own safety.

Very.

Maybe we weren't comrades after all. Maybe it was impossible to put our past behind us and to forget the hurt, the jealousy, and the complete disruption of our lives.

And this, a defiant shrug, coming from the woman who'd slept with my husband, back when he and I were still trying to work things out, back when I still loved him, back when I needed him most.

I snapped.

Literally. I knew the bitch within me helped me to snap. Gave me just the right amount of hate to fuel what I did next...and what I did next would horrify me later.

But it didn't horrify me now. Oh, no, what I did now felt just right.

So very, very right.

***

When I was done feeding from her neck, I was tempted to kill her. Tempted, of course, by the demon within me.

Instead, through superhuman effort—or,

perhaps, supernatural effort—I pulled away from her torn throat, wiping my mouth like the ghoul I am. Then I licked the back of my hand.

Yeah, definitely a monster.

Kill her, chanted a voice in my head, a voice way, way, *way* down deep. A voice I never, ever trusted. Until now, I had done such a damn good job of ignoring her, too. So good that I almost, *almost*, thought I was normal. Especially with the two rings I now wore: one that helped me to eat normal food, and one that helped me to live in the light of day. Both rings, of course, were created and forged in an alchemical process that few on Earth would ever know.

I had made a valiant attempt to not feed from humans over these past few months—or to even feast from anything living. My sole source of sustenance had been my bloody packets of filth delivered from a slaughterhouse.

Now, as I sat back, I watched Nancy sort of come back to her senses. I had seen this before. Victims slipped into a catatonic state of shock, I assumed. Allison never had, though, when I'd fed from her each week. Perhaps a friendly bite to eat was much different than a full-fledged vampire attack.

And I had attacked Nancy, too. Criminal charges could be pressed against me. *Hell, I should be in jail for what I just did to her.*

Except that no jail could hold me.

She blinked and I saw the tears roll down her cheeks. She came back to her senses slowly. Jesus, had I put her under a sort of spell? *The way a dolphin stuns its prey with a sonic blast.* She rolled her head in my direction. More tears streamed out. The wound in her neck had already coagulated, although it still seeped some blood.

I tried to feel really bad about what I had done.

The old me would have been mortified. The old me would have hated herself for attacking this woman. The old me would have feared that such an attack would prompt more such attacks, that it would, in fact, signal the end of my humanity.

The old me was a wuss.

Besides, humanity was overrated.

Yes, I knew that was *her* talking, the demon within. But sometimes, she made sense. And sometimes, people just deserved what they got. And sometimes, I just needed to feed.

All good points, I thought.

I knew I was slipping. I knew the demon within me was gaining a stronger foothold, gaining more and more access to my thoughts... and to my actions. There was a war raging within me, and I was losing ground. The enemy was advancing.

And I didn't care.

***

"Are you okay, Sam?"

I had erased her memory of the attack, of course. Under the circumstances, it seemed the prudent thing to do. With a few well-placed words and a suggestion that the past few minutes had never happened, I was in the clear. There was some blood on her shirt, but I'd suggested to her that the blood was from an old scratch that had since healed.

"Yes, I'm fine," I said, my thoughts shielded deep behind an impregnable wall.

"Okay, good. You sort of got this funny look on your face..." Nancy said.

"And then?"

"And then, I asked how you were doing." She laughed. "Look, I'm sorry if I pushed any buttons. I never thought we would be friends, either. It just sort of fell into our laps...and felt, well, it felt comfortable. All that other stuff...we were different people then. I didn't know you. You didn't know me. Danny was playing us both. I'm glad we can see past all that and be friends."

I tried to smile and might have even succeeded. I took in a lot of useless air and, with the guilt setting in, thought, *Yeah, some friend I am*.

***

"You attacked her?"

"A little bit," I underreported to my psychic friend, Allison. We were having lunch at Lazy Dog in Brea, a place that allowed customers to bring their dogs on the patio. I didn't own a dog, which was probably a good thing. We didn't want Fido to go missing like my neighbor's cat. "And could you say that a little louder?"

"I'm Latina," she said. "We're loud, deal with it."

"I'd rather not."

Allison shrugged and shoved a forkful of her iceberg wedge salad in her mouth. I might not be much of a salad expert—especially after not eating the stuff for over seven years—but iceberg wedge salad looked like a lazy-man's version of a regular salad.

"It's all about presentation," said Allison, picking up on my thoughts, which, nowadays, just about anyone seemed to do—at least, anyone with any kind of connection to me.

Allison's connection just happened to be stronger than just about anyone's, since, well, up to a few months ago, I'd been ingesting her blood on a regular basis. Consensually, of course. Her willingness to provide me with small snacks of human blood had a happy side effect of enhancing her psychic abilities. So, our give-and-take arrangement was quite symbiotic.

"It's all about marketing," I said, not impressed with the presentation of the salad.

"Or that, too. But I'm confused, Sam—"

"Confused about why you paid ten bucks for a side salad?"

"Never mind that, and this is much more than a side salad...it's an experience."

I snorted. Damn loudly, too.

"Anyway," said Allison, with tons of emphasis on the 'any' part. "I thought you had, you know, kicked the fresh blood habit." She looked at me hopefully. She was more than willing to go back to our old arrangement, but feeding the beast within me fresh blood had only created a bigger problem for me. A nearly uncontrollable problem.

"I don't think I can kick the habit. I can only deny myself. Anyway, this attack on Nancy wasn't so much about a need to feed, but to..."

"Hurt her?"

"Yeah," I said. "I wanted to hurt her. To lash

out at her. To finally..."

I let my voice trail off. No matter. Allison was there to pick up on my thoughts, as surely as if I had spoken them.

"To finally hurt the woman who had hurt you."

I nodded, and felt like crap. Allison, of course, had only been a willing participant for my blood hunger. I had never attacked her or torn her up. When I had fed from Allison, it was more like...sipping a fine wine. It was never... violent.

"I think," I said, as I worked through my feelings about Nancy, "that it was going to happen, one way or another, eventually."

"I'm not following."

"I had imagined doing just that to her—so many times, so many hundreds and hundreds of times. Maybe even a thousand or two. There was a lot of momentum behind those feelings. I'm not sure if I could have stopped myself. It was almost as if I had to act it out, just to get it out of my system."

"Okay, I think I'm following," said Allison, nodding. "Like you attracted it or something? What do those hippy-dippies call it...manifested? You manifested it."

"I guess," I said. "But on the bright side, I didn't tear her head off and punt it over my back fence into the Pep Boys parking lot, which I had been imagining, too."

Allison cocked an eyebrow at me. "Well, hopefully, it's out of your system now."

"Hopefully."

"Sam..."

"How the hell am I supposed to know how this works? One minute she's giving me sass, and the next I'm tearing through her throat and gorging on her blood so fast that it almost came out my nose. I didn't exactly plan on doing it, you know. It was impulsive."

"I know, Sam. But remember last time..."

I nodded. The last time I had fed from something living, I had torn it to pieces. The aforementioned neighbor's cat. My hunger had been fueled by the entity within me, an entity I had permitted to grow stronger by doing just that: giving her fresh blood.

I knew better now, which was why I fed from clear plastic packets of filthy cow and pig blood. And I didn't feed as often, or as much. Just enough to sustain myself. Just enough to keep my energy up, but not so much that it empowered her.

It was a fine balance, but one I had been straddling successfully for the past few months, despite my urges, my hungers.

"You're going to have to be careful, Sam.

Keep her dormant. Keep her weak."

"I know," I said, knowing that Allison was talking about the entity inside of me. "Now, can we quit making me feel like shit and get back to why you hate money?" I pointed at her salad.

"Hate money, how? Never mind. I get it. I hate money because I overspent on my salad..."

"Boy, did you ever."

***

I was thirty minutes into some heavy traffic when my business appointment canceled on me. Via text.

I briefly considered going over there anyway and canceling my prospective client's face, until I realized that didn't make a whole lot of sense. Still, it was a nice thought, whatever it was.

No, I thought. *That's* her *thinking.*

I had let the genie out of the bottle, so to speak. Or, in this case, the demonic bitch. I had fed her human blood, and not from a willing and calm participant. With my violent attack on Nancy, I had given the dark bitch inside of me a renewed strength and hope and life...and that was never, ever a good thing. I had fed...*evil.*

Now, as I sat in traffic, I briefly considered how I could have gone about things differently with Nancy. The anger I had felt had risen up quickly. Had I even had time to talk myself down? I didn't know. It had all happened so quickly. A sudden rage. A vicious attack. A gluttonous feeding from a pulsing throat.

Get up, I told myself now, *and walk away. Better than attacking. Better than losing it all. And better than giving the entity within any life at all.*

There was a tiny break in the traffic as people bailed off the nearest ramp, even crowding the dirt shoulder in their eagerness to get off this tedious stop-and-go parade of exhaust-belching cars. There was no way I was getting off into that neighborhood. I inched my car forward, maybe five feet.

Oh, joy, I thought.

I idly considered abandoning my vehicle on the side of the road and taking flight...except that I had never taken flight with Talos during the day. Would he even come? Could I transform? Did I need the silent magic of night to make the transition? I didn't know, but I figured that someday I would find out.

I looked down at my phone and really wasn't very surprised to see a restricted call. Who the restricted call was from was anybody's guess...but I had my suspicions.

"Moon Investigations," I said, making the effort to use my hands-free headset to answer so

I wouldn't get a ticket.

"Samantha, it's Ted with the California State Parks."

"Ranger Ted," I said, my suspicions confirmed. We had met in the ranger station just outside Arrowhead. They now kept me on speed dial, ever since I had helped to bring home a sheriff's missing wife a few months ago, a wife who wasn't so much missing as she'd been held captive by a pack of werewolves. Long story. Ranger Ted, of course, didn't know about the werewolf part, which was how I intended to keep it. Anyway, I'd also helped find a missing camp counselor and an arsonist.

My phone vibrated with another text. I looked down and saw that it was Nancy Pearson. Okay, maybe I was getting a little too close to my deceased ex-husband's mistress. Chatting once or twice every few months seemed perfectly reasonable. But now, we were text message buddies? I ignored her text.

"Are they still keeping you hopping over there?" I said into the headset.

"Hopping? Yeah, that, too," Ted said. "Got a minute?"

"I'm stuck on the 91 Freeway, what do you think?"

"Even on a Saturday?"

"Even on a Saturday," I said.

"You see, this is why I work in the woods. No traffic in the woods, other than a few drunken yahoos and..."

"And what?"

"Poachers," he said.

"Poachers?" I repeated.

"Right."

"On the king's land?" I asked, shocked.

He didn't laugh at my sarcasm. "No, in the forest. We've found two dead bucks, field-dressed, and with their heads removed. They're trophy hunters—for the antlers—and apparently, they wanted the meat, too, and might be coming back for it."

"Are you telling me this to make me vomit up my Mango-A-Go-Go Jamba Juice?" I said, to try to sound as normal as possible. Truth was, I found his description very intriguing. *Too intriguing.*

It's the bitch in me. Such a sicko.

"Sorry about the mango-whatever-you-just-said, but we need a good man—or woman—working the case. I'm stretched too thin with the forest fires on the north side. You interested?"

"Usual pay?" I asked.

"Another year," he said, referring to my free national park pass.

"And how many am I at, now?"

"Four, I think. Non-transferable, of course."

"Of course," I said. "I'll swing by tomorrow morning."

"On a Sunday?" He sounded impressed.

"The poachers," I told Ted. "That's when they'll come back for the meat. If they field-dressed the carcass, they'll be back before the flies lay eggs in it."

"You're right," he said.

Now that I knew I had the day off, thanks to my canceling potential client, I wanted to be with the kids today.

"See you then."

Traffic inched forward.

It was about ten minutes after we clicked off that I remembered Nancy Pearson's text message. It was another two minutes before I decided to actually read it while traffic was at a complete standstill.

He's going to kill me, Sam. At working house. Please help...anything. He's here now. Shit, don't call

Don't call. She was hiding. She was hiding right now. Or possibly hurt. Right now. Or even dead. Right now. All because I was too pissy to pick up my cell and look at her message.

The working house.

Yeah, I knew the place. It was a small home around the corner from my dead hubby's strip club, a house where some of the girls serviced some of the customers...the high-roller customers. Nancy had described it to me. I had a vague idea of where it was. Vague was all I needed.

I looked at the traffic, looked at the text, and pulled over to the side of the road. I slipped between the two front seats and settled along the messy back bench...and closed my eyes.

And summoned the single flame.

***

I appeared in the alley behind the strip club.

I could do that: appear and disappear—or teleport, as Allison called it. Apparently, it was a rare gift among vampires. I had seen it used by the oldest vampire of all, Dracula, no less. I had watched him appear and disappear on command, masterfully, perfectly, and wipe out a clan of werewolves in the process.

I wasn't quite that good...yet. *But that's the thing with immortals: we have all the time in the world.*

One prerequisite was that I needed to know where I was teleporting. *I might be undead, but appearing inside of a wall has got to hurt.*

Now, as I appeared in the alleyway, I prayed like hell that there wasn't a parked truck here, and that I didn't manifest under its hood.

I was lucky this time. I appeared whole and intact and not as part of a combustible engine. The alley was mostly empty, except for a guy who had been looking through the Dumpster. Now, of course, he was running like a man who had just seen a woman appear in front of him out of thin air.

I grinned and headed for the house around the corner.

***

There were many houses around the corner, unfortunately. All small and surrounded by low metal fences.

I paused on the sidewalk, under the blazing sun, feeling weaker than I wanted to feel. I cast my thoughts in an ever-widening gyre, far enough out to see into the homes around me. *Yeah, I can do that, too.*

The neighborhood was quiet. The homes were close together. A man attacking a woman would have been heard by any number of nearby witnesses.

On a positive note, I was pleased when I realized that I genuinely cared about Nancy's well-being. Granted, she wasn't exactly priority number one. Hell, I was happy that I cared enough to come out here. The realization told me that I wasn't a monster, and that I could, in fact, keep the monster in check.

Love, I thought again, shaking my head at the insanity of it all, as I stepped up onto her front porch. But it did make sense. Fight hate with love. Good versus evil and all of that.

I liked to think I was on the side of good.

There, the house to the left, was the closest house, in fact, to the strip club. The interior was in disarray, and I had seen blood.

I dashed off.

***

The door was locked.

That was, until I lifted my foot and kicked it in. Okay, not that I wanted to alarm this sleepy neighborhood, a neighborhood that was used to crime; a neighborhood, I suspected, that had learned to shut and lock its doors and windows and wrought-iron driveway gates.

I pushed the broken door all the way open, as the splintered wood from the doorframe caved inside.

The smell of blood and brains was strong. Almost too strong for even me to handle. The demon within me perked up, but I stamped her back in her place.

As the stench grew stronger, I stepped over a broken picture frame and drops of blood. And there was a bloody hammer neatly propped up in the far corner of the wall.

I found something else propped up in the next room, which was the kitchen. There, wedged between the refrigerator and the blood-covered cupboard, was the woman my ex-husband had cheated on me with.

It had been a clean shot with the hammer that had caved in her skull. *One bash*, I thought.

She had died, I assumed, instantly.

Her spirit was nowhere to be seen, which wasn't necessarily rare. It just meant that she had moved on, much faster than most.

I stood over her, and stared down at her bulging eyes and blood-covered thighs and down into the hole at the top of her head.

The thing within me was interested in the corpse and all the blood, but the thing within me could go to hell.

I'm not psychic, nor do I want to be.

I had enough weird shit to contend with. I also didn't want to have to deal with knowing the future, or even the past.

And so, I stood there, looking down at the corpse of a woman who had, I thought, loved my deceased ex-husband. She was a woman who had done her best to befriend me and to make things right. And she was a woman who was still turning tricks, despite my pleas for her to give it up.

'Easy money,' she had said.

Maybe I'm more psychic than I thought.

There were only a few who knew of this house, and who would use it:

The strip club's elite customers. The politicians, the lawyers, the judges, and—*dare I think it*—the cops.

A club that my ex-husband had once owned provided top-tier clients with privacy for their dalliances. It was a strip club that would have, believe it or not, reverted to our kids, had the world known that Danny was really dead. I idly wondered if he had had a share of what the women earned in the working house. I shook my head. No, even Danny wouldn't have gone that low. I hoped not, anyway.

The world, of course, only assumed he was missing, or was maybe on the lam from a debt, which was how I wanted to keep it. The world didn't need to know that he was buried in a cavern under the Los Angeles River, along with two vampires.

A long story that was best kept secret.

I nodded, feeling fury build within me. Yeah, I cared about Nancy. I cared a whole helluva lot. And now, she was dead.

I turned and dashed through the broken door...

And headed to the strip club.

***

It was midday and, as a creature of the night, I wasn't yet at full strength.

However, I had feasted on Nancy just the day before—just the day before she had been killed.

Bad week for Nancy, I thought, as I came up to the strip club's back exit, the very exit that I suspected Nancy and her killer had used, what, twenty to thirty minutes ago.

The door was locked but not for long. So far, I'd yet to come across a lock that could keep me out. Or any vampire, for that matter. And, no, I didn't need to be invited in. When would I ever get any shopping done? Or go anywhere, for that matter? Who would invite me into a mall? Or the gas station? Thank God that little factoid had been debunked. It was bad enough that I couldn't see myself in a mirror. I didn't want to have Anthony running into the Walmart or Target to get the managers to invite me in, too.

I paused and scanned my surroundings and made sure no one was standing directly behind the door. The space was empty. Good thing, because when I was done kicking the door in, the whole thing slammed back in a clanging cloud of dust.

To hell with invitations, I thought, and stepped into the strip club.

***

The crashing door got the attention of two strippers, both of whom came rushing out of a side room, and both of whom were bouncing in places—never mind.

I pointed to their changing rooms and they stared at me, then at each other, then bounced off into the changing rooms and slammed their doors shut.

At least they're street-smart, I thought, and pushed through the back hallway.

Music thumped. Lights flashed. And on the stage was a completely nude, skinny, tattooed girl whose mother and father probably wept into their pillows at night. The lights were focused on the stage, around which one-dollar bills had been tossed, with the occasional fiver thrown in for good luck. Or a hope for more of a show.

It was midday—hell, not even one p.m.—and the strip club was nearly half full.

Ever the optimist, I thought, and surveyed

the room. The stage itself was encircled with hundreds of white lights, which alternately flashed. Classy.

I'd been here before, back when I had applied for a job—long story—and I knew the layout fairly well. The layout wasn't much: in the center, a raised stage. Single brass pole. Chairs circling the stage, filled with bored, albeit mildly turned-on, middle-aged men with nothing to lose. The girl on stage was completely nude, gleaming with sweat and looked, unbelievably, like she was enjoying herself. Dancing and cavorting and slinking and spreading, she seemed, well, into it.

Like they say, love what you do.

I shook my head and continued surveying the room. No one took an interest in me. *Maybe because I had clothes on.* The Hispanic bartender leaned a hip against the back counter and watched the dancing girl. If I had to guess, his mind was elsewhere. Working here, day after day, night after night, year after year, how many naked women had he seen? How many had it taken him to begin losing interest? Or, was it even possible for a guy to see too many naked women? I didn't know, but the blank stare on his face suggested that it might be a possibility.

I continued scanning. Rick, who was the

manager of the joint, was at the bar, his back turned to the dancer. Rick had, I think, the thickest neck I had ever seen. Even thicker than Kingsley's.

There were, maybe, twenty customers. Most were seated around the stage. A handful were in the back booths. Single guys, sitting alone. Not talking. Hating themselves but interested in naked flesh even more.

From the back room to my right and from a dark corner, emerged a man with short, slicked-back dark hair, a man who, from all appearances, looked freshly cleaned up. Refreshed, even. He nodded to a bouncer type who was standing guard outside what I knew to be the private rooms. Or the sex rooms. The big guy returned his nod. The two looked, well, like they had a secret. I doubted the big black guy knew the secret extended all the way back to a murdered stripper in the house next door. I suspected the big bouncer had arranged for Nancy and this guy to be alone just outside of the club...and by arranged, I meant paid nicely.

But as I watched the exchange, growing admittedly more interested by the second, I noticed two things: the guy with the short black hair had his dark shirt on inside-out.

Oh, and he didn't sport an aura of any kind.

He was, I was certain, a vampire.

***

As he slid into the back seat, I could smell it now. Fresh blood, wafting from his direction. His shirt, I suspected, was covered with the stuff.

Nancy's blood.

Before overreacting, I reminded myself that I had spilled that same blood.

No, I thought. *Not spilled. Drank. Deeply. Violently. Angrily.*

In fact, I had taken a decisive step backward from all the progress I had made these past few months. I had reined in the demon bitch nicely, and for that I was grateful. The less fresh blood she had, the weaker she became. That's the way I liked it. That's the way it had been for many years after the initial attack that had turned me. Since then, I had drunk only the putrid cow and pig blood. I had inadvertently kept her at bay with the least-desirable sustenance I could find.

That was, until the first killing. The gangbanger who had wanted to gang rape me was my first blood. That hadn't ended too well for the young man.

Still, I reminded myself, I hadn't killed Nancy. I had only...partaken of her. And awakened a slumbering giant within myself. In fact, I felt her rising up through my consciousness now. She sensed, as well as I did, that the shit was about to hit the fan.

And she wanted a front-row seat.

Well, I thought. *Enjoy the ride.*

I moved away from the back doorway, and headed behind the stage and to the sated vampire who, even now, was watching me come to him.

With a smile on his face.

***

I took the seat opposite him, my back to the stage. I was missing the performance of the girl who danced like no one was watching—except, of course, most of the pervs in Colton were doing exactly that.

The chair seemed unstable, and I wondered how many lap dances it had endured. And with that thought alone, I vomited a little in the back of my mouth.

The man with the slicked-back hair wasn't a man. He wasn't a werewolf either. He seemed too slight. The werewolves I had seen were big boys...growing bigger, in fact, with each full moon. The older the werewolf, the bigger he was. Which made Kingsley one of the oldest, I realized.

And hairiest, I thought.

"You killed Nancy." My voice came out flat, emotionless, even.

"Oh, was that her name?" He hadn't blinked yet. Oldest trick in the book. I could out-unblink the crap out of him. He kept his wide-eyed stare on me. His skin, I saw, was flushed. He had had a healthy feeding, of course. After all, why waste all that good blood? I, of course, hadn't had anything all day...and the Jamba juice didn't count. At least, not for my kind.

Whatever kind I was, that is.

A vampire, I told myself. *A vampire, for once and for all.*

Except, of course, I didn't really believe that. I never did. I wasn't so much a vampire as a person who was possessed by a very, very dark and powerful entity, an entity whose own supernatural powers leaked through.

No, not leaked...poured through.

And the guy in front of me seemed too fresh, too excited, too happy. He seemed, in fact, to revel in exactly what he was.

He's a new vampire.

Which bode well for me. The older the vamps, I noticed, the stronger they were...and the more aware of the powers they possessed. New vamps relied on strength only. At least, I had.

Except, early on, I had had my early warning system, a slight ringing in my head which was, even now, sounding strongly... warning the crap out of me.

"Yes," I said, "and she was a friend of mine." And she *had* been a friend, dammit. Even if only for the past few months.

He said, "You should turn around and pretend you never saw me."

"Or not."

Oh, yeah. This guy was new, and a little full of himself. And, judging by the damage he had inflicted on Nancy, a certifiable psychopath. Not to mention, he couldn't see auras—at least, not yet. Had he been able to, he would have seen what I was. No matter.

"Leave now, and I won't kill you, too," he said casually.

"How many others have you killed?" I asked.

He tilted his head a little. Still didn't blink. Still a little too full of himself. If I had to guess, he probably had posters of Tom Cruise as Lestat on his bedroom walls, and probably a poster or two of Damon from *The Vampire Diaries*, too.

"You wanted to be a vampire all your life, and now, you are one, and you think it gives you a license to kill. Except, asshole, some of the people you are going to kill are going to be friends with other people, people who are not really people, but similar to your own kind."

Finally, he blinked, and that might have been my greatest victory yet.

"You're one, too," he said, after a moment, piecing it together.

"Lucky for you, being a vamp doesn't require an admissions test."

"Well, then, I am sorry about your friend. If it's any consolation to you, she was delicious."

"That's a shitty thing to say about someone I cared about."

"Then, that's your problem, you care too—"

"Cut *The Vampire Diaries* angst, asshole. This is the real world and you just killed a friend of mine, and, I suspect, you have killed others like her. *And*, I suspect, you are going to keep doing this to people until someone puts you in the ground with a silver stake through your heart."

He blinked again, and again, and I believe he saw that I might have been serious. And that he might be hip-deep in some serious shit.

"So, what do you propose we do?" he asked.

"I propose that *you* stop killing innocent people, for starters."

"She was hardly innocent. She was just a who—"

"Don't say it," I said. "Remember that part

about her being my friend."

"You know, who are you? Fuck you and fuck your whore friend. I just wish I hadn't killed her so quickly."

He was bigger than me. Physically, I had no doubt he was stronger. By how much, I didn't know. *I'm not the oldest vampire. Hell, I'm relatively new to this stuff, too.*

Except...well, except I had some mad skills.

I saw the flame, and a blink later, I was by his side. He gasped and turned and reached for me. Except I already had a hold on his arm.

The flame again, and this time, we disappeared together...

Only to reappear somewhere that I was very familiar with. In fact, I had investigated a murder scene out here...in the desert outside of Corona.

The *open* desert. Where there was no shade.

We both stumbled and fell. After all, we had been sitting in the strip club when we'd disappeared.

We both stood up about the same time, although only one of us looked shocked and horrified and, well, hot as hell. His skin, I noticed, was already smoking.

I dusted myself off, pointed to the sun above, nodded, and disappeared just as he lunged for me.

It's good to be me.
Sucks to be him.

***

It was late, and I was waiting. Impatiently.

There were times when I didn't like Nancy. In fact, if I would added up all the time I had spent hating her, it would far outweigh the time I, well, tolerated her. But she had made the effort to see me, the effort to connect, and, dammit, there had been something there. A spark. I was sorry to see her go.

Whether or not the vampire in the desert had made it out alive, I didn't know, but I doubted it. He was as good as dead, and I didn't feel much sympathy for him at all. And the entity within him would simply depart, only to find another host. A very sick circle indeed.

The entity within me, throughout the course of the day, had mostly settled back into the darkest corners of my mind, where she would stay, waiting for more blood, waiting for more pain, and waiting, also, for a special someone.

That special someone had yet to make another appearance, but I often sensed him nearby, watching me. Waiting for me. Waiting for me to...what? I didn't know. Come around, perhaps. After all, her special someone was special, indeed...none other than the Count himself. I just happened to like the guy, which made me question who and what I was all over again.

I checked the time on my phone again. 3:22 a.m. When did these places close down, anyway?

I didn't know, but by now, there were only a few cars left in the parking lot.

At 3:45, the last car drove away. I recognized the silhouette of the thick neck of Rick, the manager, as his car receded down the street. I used my vampire senses to see if anyone was still inside the strip club. *Empty.*

That was also the time I got out of my minivan, which I'd discreetly parked down the street. With a spring in my step, I approached the strip club, carrying the can of gasoline by my side.

***

It didn't take me long to dowse the structure with gasoline. That I did so with a surprising glee should have been alarming. I never knew I had such an inner arsonist.

I stood a few dozen feet away, and held up the fancy lighter I'd purchased at a smoke shop for just this occasion.

The strip club had brought so much pain to my life. The strip club had been the beginning of the end of my relationship with Danny.

I hated the strip club, even if it had brought an unlikely friend into my life. The friendship had been bumpy and likely would have remained so. I likely would never have truly forgiven her, but I had been willing to try, and so had she.

Either way, it was time to close this chapter of my life...

In a grand fashion.

I held up the lighter, flicked it to life, and tossed it into a nearby pool of gasoline.

The End

Moon Love

Chapter One

"It's a cabin," I said.

"Not just any cabin," said Kingsley, dropping our suitcases just inside the door. "It's our Valentine's weekend getaway cabin. Which means..."

"I know, I know," I said. "It means it's magical. You told me."

Kingsley stepped beyond the foyer, rubbing his hands together in anticipation of such 'magic' as he moved under a rough-hewn beam from which potted ferns hung. He looked up, ooh-ing and ah-ing. I looked up, too, although I didn't ooh and I certainly didn't ah. The log cabin was spacious and open and well-lit. Most of the light came from the floor-to-ceiling window that overlooked a lot of forest and the bright blue lake beyond.

He said, "It's going to be the rarest kind of magic, Sam. This is a kid-free, vampire-free, werewolf-free, monster-free, work-free, kid-free zone—"

"You already said kid-free—"

"Shh, Sam," he said, appearing at my side far faster than the hulking bastard ever should be able to move. "Mostly, this is a no-worry zone."

"Fine," I said. "Except, how are we going to escape the no-vampire and no-werewolf part? Last I checked, I have a penchant for blood, and you have a penchant for sniffing butts."

Kingsley shook his head and laughed a little too loudly. The sound of it echoed throughout the Big Bear cabin, itself nearly eight thousand feet above nearby Orange County, where we both worked and played—though I didn't do much playing these days. Not with two kids, one of whom is a telepathic teenager with a rebellious streak, and the other, a budding superhero who is as strong as a moose. Well, a young moose.

"Now, Sam. We agreed: No talk of anything paranormal, abnormal, supernatural, unnatural, preternatural, metaphysical, non-physical, weird, freaky or downright not right."

This had been his mantra all *freaking* week. Enough! It had been emailed, texted, and voice-noted. Voice notes were still new to me, but the hairy bastard loved to leave me long-winded notes, which came through as text message alerts with a "play" button attached. Cute, but gimmicky.

I'll admit, despite all of Kingsley's efforts for a relaxing weekend, and despite all his planning and attention to detail, I was in a bit of a mood. I'd had it up to here—that is, up to my five-foot, three-inch frame—of just how darn wonderful this weekend was going to be. He'd promised I was going to be wined, dined and cloud-nined. I knew what he really meant: a wonderful kid-free weekend. Meaning, free of *my* kids, since the big oaf hadn't sired any of his own yet.

(And how he'd managed to escape seeding the world with hairy, oversized kids, I didn't know. The man had been a world-class playboy. Maybe he shot blanks. Maybe werewolves were sterile. Maybe he'd practiced safe sex, using massive, custom-made, Teflon-clad condoms. I wondered again if the big meatball could get me pregnant, or if I could even *get* pregnant. Maybe since I turned vamp, I, too, was sterile.)

He'd stipulated a work-free weekend, too. Hell, he even made me sign a legal agreement that I would not work any cases for precisely three days. I had signed it just to get him off my back, and because the agreement was kind of cute, too. Of course, my signature had read: "Bite me."

Truth was, I had a full caseload. More than

full. I was busy as hell, and not with sexy cases. Lots of background checks, cheating spouses, and process serving, all of which I did to pay the bills. But, yes, this was Valentine's weekend, and I wanted to be a good girlfriend. I also wanted to pay my mortgage, since having a place to call home is always nice, but I'd put my work on hold and decided to go along for this little misadventure, er, weekend getaway. Had I said no, well, there would have been a lot of whimpering. And not the cute kind from puppies. The grating kind from a full-grown, butt-hurt werewolf. Of the two of us, he was the romantic. Go figure.

"Fine," I said, crossing my arms, maybe a little too tightly and defensively. "No talk of things that go bump in the night—or of my kids, whom, apparently, you hate."

Okay, maybe I was the butt-hurt one.

Kingsley took one of my hands and untangled my arms. He held it in his big, warm paw. That he towered over me by nearly a foot-and-a-half should have been off-putting, but it wasn't. Not with him. He was exactly the right size, as far as I was concerned. I loved the way his long hair just reached down to me, or that it enveloped me completely when he held me close. I loved that Kingsley was bigger and badder than just about anyone, ever. The private eye in Huntington Beach was a close second, but he didn't have shoulders like Kingsley, nor the sheer amount of muscle mass.

"I adore your kids, Sammie. You know that."

"Well, you mentioned them twice in your little run-down of terrible things not to talk about this weekend."

"And I also mentioned us. Or, rather, our kind. After all, one of us is a bloodsucker, and the other, apparently, likes to sniff butts."

"Don't make me laugh," I said. "Not when I'm mad at you."

"Mad at me… why?"

"Because you think my kids get in the way. You knew I had kids. You knew what you were signing up for when you availed me of your werewolf charms."

"I love your kids, Sam. I really do."

This was, of course, the first time he had said those words. About my kids. I pulled back. "You do?"

"Sam, I know I don't say it enough, and certainly, I haven't said it to them, but you're damn straight I love those little freaks."

I punched his shoulder, hard enough to hurt. At least, hurt anyone who wasn't the size of a Macy's Thanksgiving Day Parade float. He laughed and rubbed his shoulder. "Those little fists can do damage."

"You have no idea."

"I have some idea. Now, are we good?"

"So, you really love them?" I asked.

"Your little fists? Yes, they're very cute—ouch!"

I had punched him again. "My kids, furball."

He chuckled and held my hands in his and looked down at me with those big, beautiful, intense amber eyes. He nodded once, twice, and said, "Yeah, Sam. I really do love them."

I had no idea why those words were so important for me to hear or why they had brought me to tears, but they were and they had. I buried my face deep inside the crook of his arm, while he held me close enough to smother me in his bulky embrace. Thank God I didn't need to breathe.

Chapter Two

We were on our way into town for dinner.

These days, dinner was a bigger deal for me, for which I was eternally grateful. Dinner meant I could hold down my food, drink an array of beverages, and even have dessert. That my body needed none of it, well, that was another story. Or that some of the food had lost its flavor was a sad story I mostly kept to myself. Eating out was fun in and of itself, a chance to connect, to explore, to consume, and to spend Kingsley's money. Something of a gourmand, he never took me out for cheap eats. It was always to the finest places that served high-end meat. And lots of it.

Big Bear Lake is picturesque and often breathtaking, with the bluest man-made lake imaginable. A long lake, it sat eight thousand feet high, nestled in what must have once been a ravine. Now, homes surrounded it, some of which were quite large.

Apparently, Big Bear was a getaway for the rich and famous, too. I wasn't rich or famous, but Kingsley did rather well. Anyway, the blue expanse of water was a far cry from the desert lake I'd recently been exposed to, both above and below its surface. Where Lake Elsinore did all it could to cling to life in the deserts of Southern California, Big Bear Lake seemed at home up here in the mountains, as if it had been here all along, as if it had been meant to be here, and that man had only given it a goose, so to speak. Of course, Lake Elsinore had the added benefit of boasting an honest-to-God lake monster. What lurked beneath the surface of Big Bear Lake remained to be seen.

We rounded a bend in the road, with Kingsley driving a little too fast for my taste. That's the thing with immortals: even if he wrecked the car, and wrecked us, too, we'd still come out of the wreckage smelling like roses. Granted, I wasn't in the mood to roll off the side of the hill and into the lake below, but Kingsley seemed determined to push the limits of his Lincoln Navigator, his reflexes, and my nerves.

It was just past dusk and I was alive and alert and stronger than, seemingly, this time of day yesterday. Now, as I sat in the front seat, thrown occasionally to the right or left—like the turbulent Indiana Jones ride at Disneyland—I felt the energy of life itself coursing through me. It crackled and snapped and spread from my solar plexus and outward to my arms and legs, down into my core, filling me, filling me. I opened and closed my hands and wanted to...

crush something. I wanted to hold a can of Mountain Dew, and just smash it down into a ball. I could, too. Easily, quickly, completely. I took in air and held it and held and held it, and then released it. As I exhaled, I wondered if my earlier thought was true: did I, in fact, get stronger each day, each year? Even if minutely? Kingsley got bigger with each turning. Why couldn't I get stronger, too?

Sure, Kingsley's steady growth was his body's attempt to eventually match the size and shape of the hulking creature within him. Why couldn't that extend to me? Why couldn't I grow in strength steadily, as I eventually met the strength of the demoness within me? Which begged the question, just how strong was that bloodthirsty bitch inside me?

I thought about that as we rounded another bend on two wheels—or what felt like two wheels, hitting the kinds of G's that I'd only experienced when hurtling through the air as Talos—when I spotted the little boy walking along the side of the road.

***

He was wearing only a tee-shirt and shorts. His hands were shoved deep into his pockets. He wore socks and shoes, but he looked cold and miserable. He also looked to be about eight years old. I glanced at the dashboard temperature: 42 degrees.

"Kingsley—"

"I see him."

"Why is he walking on the side of the road?"

"Maybe he lives around here."

"And why is he wearing only a tee-shirt and shorts?"

"I don't know, Sam."

I was just about to tell him to pull over when the boy did something mystifying: he dashed off the road and plunged into the woods.

"Jesus, where did he go?"

"Like I said, maybe he lives around here. There's probably a house up on the hill."

"Yeah, maybe," I said. But I didn't like it. Not one freakin' bit.

Chapter Three

It bothered me all through dinner.

We were at an Indian place called Himalaya. The fact that I could even eat Indian food again was a small miracle that was presently lost on me.

"He's going to be fine, Sam," said Kingsley for the dozenth time.

"I should have gone after him," I said, playing with my *matar paneer*, a spicy cheese-and-peas dish that still delivered some flavor to my degrading taste buds. Why my taste buds had decided to slowly switch off, I didn't know. But over the past year or so, food was losing its flavor, although hemoglobin was as delicious as ever. It was as if the bitch within just couldn't ever let me be happy.

"Go after him? And what? Scare him half to death? That was a busy road. How do you know the kid wouldn't have done something stupid—like run out into traffic?"

He was right, although the kid had disappeared into the forest, and hadn't shown any signs of slowing down.

"Who was he running from?" I asked.

"I don't know if he was running from someone, Sam."

I shook my head and dropped my fork. "He was. Something happened and he took off running without a jacket or pants. He was dressed for summer."

"Or maybe he was visiting a nearby friend—"

"No," I said, cutting him off. "No parent—no mother—would have let him leave without warmer clothing."

"Kids are pretty hardy up here, Sam. Their forty-three degrees is like our sixty-three."

"Do you have any idea how stupid that sounds?"

"Yeah. I heard it as soon as it left my mouth. Look, Sam. Is there any way we can just have a romantic night out?"

I looked at him. He looked at me, then nodded. "Do it."

I pulled out my cell phone and dialed 9-1-1.

Chapter Four

Big Bear Village was lined with boutique stores, restaurants, taverns, hotels and coffee shops. All of it is packaged neatly along a side street, just off the main drag. A massive arch spanned the street, welcoming anyone to the Village, and, on the reverse side, thanking them for shopping. The street itself descended down to the lake and a small harbor, within which charter boats are moored, along with a big paddlewheel tour boat.

We joined the throng of tourists and couples, all here to enjoy the Valentine's Day weekend —none of whom were worried about a little boy lost in the woods. If anything happened to that boy, I would never forgive myself. Ever.

"He's going to be okay, Sam," said Kingsley, after I failed to comment or show any interest in anything. "He's probably home with his family, getting an earful from his mother for not wearing a jacket."

I wanted to believe him. I wanted to believe the police had checked out the scene, and returned the boy home. Or helped him.

I squeezed Kingsley's hand and had just decided to start enjoying myself, if possible, when my cell phone rang. I dug it out of my front pocket, looked at the faceplate: Restricted. It was the police.

Chapter Five

We saw the flashing lights.

Kingsley pulled over along the side of the road. I hopped out before the SUV had come to a full stop, dodged some of the slow-moving, looky-loo traffic, and headed for a group of officers. Kingsley was right behind me.

Already there were a dozen local police and a handful of county sheriff's deputies. Ten squad cars in total, along with two firetrucks. Three of the officers were focused on a weeping woman. A man stood next to her, his face grim and determined, his eyes haunted. *The parents.*

The lead detective pulled us aside and asked us to tell him everything we knew. We were, of course, the last witnesses to see the boy. As I spoke, the detective kept his eyes on Kingsley. Kingsley did the same with the detective. Two alpha males eying each other. I could have cut the testosterone in the air with one of my longish, pointed fingernails.

When I was finished, we were told the boy had left home earlier in the evening, around 4 p.m. He was only seven years old. His mother worked at home as a novelist, and later discovered her son was missing. To her horror, he had left behind his jacket and beanie cap.

(She hadn't known he was wearing shorts.) She had called the police almost immediately, only to discover two witnesses—us—had reported seeing a similar boy on the side of the road, a boy who had gone off into the forest alone. The family lived one mile from here.

Detective Hernandez grabbed a couple of officers and we hoofed it up the road, to the point where I had seen the boy plunge into the forest. Kingsley had thought it was a few feet closer, but we both agreed: this was primarily the spot.

Hernandez nodded and said that would be all; they would take over from here. He turned his back on us and gave the officers instructions. They were prepping for a full-scale search and rescue, and were waiting for a volunteer team to arrive from the nearby town of Arrowhead, along with more officers. I asked if there was anything we could do, and he said no, they would take over from here. He didn't bother to look at us.

I didn't leave, not immediately. Instead, I looked up into the steeply rising hillside, up into the tangle of branches and darkening woods, with eyes that cut through the gloom and saw what the others couldn't see. Except, I didn't see anything of promise. Only trees, undergrowth, and oddly huge boulders. No trail. No reason for a kid to be out there. Not after dark, and not in this weather.

More deputies arrived from the sheriff's department. More firefighters, too. A rescue helicopter appeared next, flying low, the *whump-whump* of the blades stirring up the smells of the forest and mixing them together in an aromatic soup of decaying earth and evergreen needles. The chopper's massive spotlight blasted stark whiteness through the darkening woods.

A local TV crew followed shortly thereafter, in a van equipped with a dish on the roof. The entire news team was dressed for cold weather in puffy, quilted jackets and knitted caps with the station's logo. All except for the reporter, whose hair was loose and blonde and blowing in the increasing wind. They started setting her up for the shoot, with the dark woods behind her. Someone handed her a microphone and her face got touched up by a makeup artist, who scurried quickly away as she shivered—the only one with cleavage showing in the stiff breeze.

I noticed a sudden traffic uptick. Concerned citizens started turning up, too, all of them armed with powerful flashlights and walking sticks. Some carried rappelling gear. Now a canine unit showed up with an SUV-full of hound dog muzzles poking through the part-open windows and dripping impressive strings of drool—I saw Kingsley turn his head when they bayed. I wondered how much canine language Kingsley could understand while in his massive human form.

He answered my unspoken question with, "They don't know jack. Not yet."

The road was turning into a fiasco. Parking opportunities along the dirt road were filling up quickly on each side, until it was difficult for two cars to pass each other without someone pulling over to yield. Cars honked, people shouted, police ordered. But through it all, I heard the sound of one mother crying. Frightened out of her mind.

I instinctively moved toward the woods. As I did so, an officer spotted me and held up his hands. "Only authorized personnel, ma'am."

Kingsley took my hand. "C'mon, Sam. We've done all we could."

As he led me to the Navigator, I looked back into the dark woods, and wondered: had we really done all we could?

Chapter Six

Back at the cabin, I paced and watched the local news, the same news reporter with the cleavage.

Kingsley was sitting on the L-shaped couch, one leg up, a highball glass of scotch in one hand. He was taking this disappearance far more lightly than I was. He had the utmost trust and respect for the local search and rescue effort and repeatedly expressed his confidence in them.

Me, not so much. I had a bad feeling about all of this.

"We have to let them do their job, Sam."

"I am," I said, pacing. "For now."

Kingsley shook his shaggy head and chuckled lightly. He was treading on dangerous ground. "These guys are trained professionals, Sam. They have maps. A canine unit. A chopper. They know every inch of that forest."

I doubted that, but bit my tongue. I knew the San Bernardino Sheriff's Department, which had made the news recently in their efforts to subdue a local terrorist threat, also patrolled the biggest county in the United States. That's right, San Bernardino County, located in the interior of Southern California, sported over twenty thousand square miles of mountains, deserts and cities, all of which a person could get hella lost in, as Tammy would say. Or used to say. Whatever. Honestly, I couldn't keep up with teenage lingo.

I continued pacing. It was now late evening, that gray area between dusk and full-blown night. It was also when I was at my strongest. I should be out there. I should be searching the woods right alongside their search and rescue crew. Hell, I had night vision, for crissakes. So did Kingsley. What were we doing in this warm cabin while the boy was out there somewhere, no doubt freezing?

I continued pacing, continued running my fingers through my hair. What the devil had that kid been up to? Why on God's green earth was he walking around in shorts and a tee-shirt, in this weather? Why had he dashed off the road and into the woods? I paused, and nearly pulled my hair out. And why the hell was the live newscast not reporting that he had been found?

Because he hadn't, of course.

Because he was still out there, alone and freezing or, worse, with someone fixing to do him harm. Yes, I'd said "fixing to." My father used to say: "fixing to." I say it, too, when I'm upset.

More pacing back and forth across the

Navajo rugs. Kachina figures on the mantel, watching me. My hands opened and closed, my pointy, sharp nails digging into my palms.

"Sam, baby, chill," said Kingsley, but he let his voice trail off, when a spokeswoman for the county sheriff walked up to a podium, for the scheduled press conference. I paused, standing in front of the TV, blocking the screen from his view, but I didn't care. I was hella annoyed with him because, had I been up here alone, the boy would have been found already because nothing and nobody would have stopped me from looking.

The news wasn't good, according to the reporter. Searchers hadn't turned up any evidence. The canine unit had picked up a promising scent trail that had been lost in a creek. The dogs hadn't picked up the scent again, not on either creek bank. The mother walked to the podium, the same woman I'd seen at the side of the road, and she was just a wreck. She begged anyone with information about her son to come forward. She begged anyone for help.

And when I heard her utter the word, "Help," I spun around to face Kingsley.

He nodded before I could. "Let's find him, Sam."

"Great—"

"But that's a big mountain, Sam. We're going to need help."

I thought about that, nodded, and pulled out my cell phone.

It was time to call in the cavalry.

Chapter Seven

It was two hours later, and they were all here. My friends kicked ass like that. Minus good ole Fang, because, well… most of my friends were cops and private dicks and psychics and witches. Fang did not play well with others. Especially law enforcement.

Two hours of agonizing waiting on this crew, mind you. But the invited were here, and they were ready. Even Allison, Spinoza and Aaron King, all of whom had just arrived from Los Angeles.

We were a group of misfits, all crowded here in the open living room with its vaulted ceilings. We needed the head space, trust me. Three of the guys—Kingsley, Knighthorse and Sanchez—all towered over the six-foot mark. Sherbet was right behind them. Even the elderly Aaron King stood right at six feet, which, I might add, was the exact height of The King himself, Elvis Presley.

Spinoza was a diminutive guy, maybe just a few inches taller than me. But he projected much bigger, especially with those brooding, haunted eyes. Sometimes I got flashes of that same haunted look in Knighthorse, but the flash quickly dispersed into his usual, cocksure self.

Detective Sanchez of the LAPD was his good friend, and a one-time client of mine, of sorts. Little had Sanchez realized that a case he'd been working on had been vampire-related. He didn't know this because I had erased his memory of it. Still, he remembered me, although he might not remember why and how he remembered me.

My life is weird like that.

Rounding out the cavalry, or the "big guns," as Knighthorse now referred to the group, were Detective Sherbet and Monty and Ellen Drew. Sherbet had brought a dozen donuts, of which four were missing upon arrival. Monty and Ellen were my friends, although I didn't see them nearly enough. Monty was a former private eye with whom I had crossed paths years ago, back when I'd worked for HUD. Now, he and his wife worked as international ghost hunters. Yes, people paid them to inspect homes and buildings, even whole towns, for ghosts. Ellen, as it turned out, was a psychic medium, which should bode well for our search tonight.

I filled them in on what I knew about the little boy; in particular, I related what I'd seen and my impressions. Knighthorse and Spinoza were lounging at the counter, a bottle of Bud Light in front of Knighthorse and a bottle of water in front of Spinoza. From what I understood, the smaller detective had sworn off all alcohol—knowing his history as I did, I didn't blame him. Knowing what he'd been through, I think he would have been hard-pressed to ever drink again.

Sherbet was leaning a meaty shoulder against the fridge, a can of Coke held loosely in his hand. Monty and Ellen sat together on the couch, flanked by Allison and Sanchez. Aaron King, with his lopsided grin and damn good looks (even for an older guy), hung out next to me. Kingsley, true to form, stood right smack-dab in the center of the kitchen, arms crossed over his massive chest, looking for all the world like Conan the Destroyer rather than Orange County's famous defense attorney.

"I don't suppose we really need a picture of the boy," said Knighthorse. "But do we have a name?"

The name hadn't been released to the general public; luckily for us, our group included two detectives who had done their homework.

"Flynn Watchtower," said Sanchez.

"Age seven and a half," added Sherbet, then shook his head. "I have no idea why I added the half part."

"Because halves are important to kids," said a soothing Ellen.

"Sure," said Sherbet. "That's why. And not

at all because of early-onset Alzheimer's."

Aaron King snorted. "I've got you by a few decades, big guy."

"Guys, guys..." I said.

"Flynn Watchtower," said the ex-football-player-now-turned-detective from Huntington Beach, shaking his big, squarish head. "Now *that's* a name. Granted, it's no Jim Knighthorse. But still..."

"Let me remind you that we have a little boy missing in the woods. The temperature is dropping, and as of only a few minutes ago, he still hasn't been found," I said.

"And according to my contact up here," said Sanchez, "they have no real leads."

"What else do they know? Besides nothing?" asked Spinoza. He seemed to be taking the news of the missing boy the hardest. Then again, Spinoza had lost his own son, for reasons he would probably never forgive himself.

"They found footprints leading up the mountain, and their bloodhounds confirmed it. But they lost their trail at a creek."

"Jesus," said Aaron King, shaking his head. "He went into the water, in this weather?"

"What can we do that the others can't?" asked Sanchez. "There are some good people out there, looking as hard as they can."

I nodded. "All of us have good instincts, or

we wouldn't be in the business we are in."

"Would you even say a sixth sense, Sam?" asked Allison, and she glanced at Ellen Drew and winked.

Knighthorse snapped his fingers. "Exactly that, but I didn't want to sound..."

"Weird?" ventured Sanchez.

"Enlightened," said Knighthorse.

Sanchez shook his head and drank more beer. I looked at Allison, and she looked at me. She stifled a grin. My eyes might have twinkled, but I wasn't in much of a mood to grin. Knighthorse—indeed, most of the men here—weren't privy to the true depth of the supernaturalism really going on in this room.

Next, I reminded everyone that for every minute we were in here, it was another minute the little boy was alone in the woods. I had found a decent two-page topographical map of the area from a Big Bear coffee table book on display in the living room. I had already ripped out the pages and taped them together.

Now, as the boys debated the likelihood of where the little guy had gone off to, pouring over the map, I pulled aside Allison and Ellen.

In the kitchen, I said to Ellen, "Are you still as psychic as ever?"

"Maybe more so."

I nodded. "More so is good. You getting any

kind of read on Flynn?"

"Something, but nothing definite. He's not afraid, that much I'm sure of."

That struck me as interesting. Allison, who worked as a telephone psychic, and who just so happened to be the real deal, nodded. "I get that, too. I get strength. Boldness. Bravado."

"Are you sure that's not all seeping in from the living room?" I asked, nodding toward the group of men who were still crowded around the map.

Ellen laughed. "Boys will be boys."

"And what about *this* boy? Flynn?" I asked. "What else are you two getting?"

"He's not in immediate danger, but..."

I waited. I had been good until Ellen had said, "but." Now, I felt sick all over again. Instantly.

"But what?" I finally asked.

"He's cold. He hadn't expected to be this cold. He knows now that going in the water was a bad idea. His clothes are wet."

"Anything else?" I asked.

"I'm seeing a cave," said Allison.

"Shallow cave," added Ellen.

"Heat," said Allison, frowning.

"Son of a bitch," said Ellen, blinking and looking me in the eye. "He just built a fire."

Chapter Eight

The plan was simple enough.

Detective Sherbet and Detective Sanchez, from the Fullerton and Los Angeles police departments, respectively, would join the official search for Flynn Watchtower, who, according to Knighthorse, sounded like a character out of *Game of Thrones.*

Speaking of which, Knighthorse and Spinoza would team up to search a location they deemed promising: a campsite about five miles from where Flynn had disappeared into the woods.

Aaron King and Monty Drew would search along the surrounding roads. Maybe, they figured, little Flynn had decided to leave the warmth of the fire and seek help along the roads.

(Yes, we told the boys of both Ellen's and Allison's psychic hits. Surprisingly, few scoffed. In fact, our biggest dissenter was Ellen's own husband, who seemed determined to wear his hat as our skeptic.)

Allison and Ellen would take to the woods, following their intuition, impressions and gut feelings. That left Kingsley and me, who would search together, using our own specialized skills.

The teams got into their respective vehicles and, armed with each other's phone numbers and shared GPS locations (apps are wonderful things), we hit the road.

Chapter Nine

The roadside was long past the fiasco stage and had now descended into pure bedlam.

Police cruisers, firetrucks, two ambulances, paramedics, three news vans, and people everywhere. Flashing lights. Concerned citizens. Looky-loos. All backing up along the side of the road, exactly where we had seen the boy run off.

It was going on 9 p.m. I had seen Flynn dart into the woods at about 5:00 p.m.

Too long for a little boy to be alone in the woods, I thought.

With the others having long ago peeled off, Kingsley drove a little further down the road, pulling over around the next bend, which was far quieter. We stepped out of the vehicle and into the cool night air. The mountain rose above, a massive, black mass, covered in proud evergreens, boulders, and sparkling, glittering light. At least, glittering to my eyes.

I looked at Kingsley, and he looked at me. We both nodded, and, like Flynn had done a few hours earlier, we plunged into the woods.

I led the way, but the wolfman was right behind me.

Chapter Ten

I ducked under branches and leaped over ferns. Kingsley crashed behind me, like the brute he was. He also kept pace with me, step for step. In fact, he began taking the lead. His eyes, I noted, were glowing particularly bright.

Two freaks, running in the woods.

Yeah, that sounded about right.

I raced along a barely-there trail, hardly more than game trail, if that. It was enough. I leaped over tall white snapdragons, dwarf pussy-toes, and dogbane—the names of which would have confirmed to Knighthorse that he really had stepped onto the set of *Game of Thrones*.

I grinned at that thought—my first real grin in many hours, and flew up the trail with a surprisingly fleet-of-foot Kingsley behind me. Too fleet of foot. I looked back and saw, with some surprise, that I was no longer being followed by my hulking, two-legged boyfriend, but by an animal of the four-legged variety.

The black wolf bounded over the trail, his tail rigid and flat, his paws bigger than any paws I'd ever seen before, his eyes flashing amber. *Yeah,* I thought, *that's not weird at all.* I turned back and picked up my pace, amazed again that I could find another gear when needed. And I found it now, flying over the trail, over saplings and bushes and boulders—all of which were a blur. As I ran, I scanned, looking for anything that resembled a cave. I was looking for firelight, too.

If there was a fire out here, I would eventually see it as a superheated blazing ball. Unlike Kingsley, I didn't have the ability to capture what little light there was, and expand it into night vision. No, I saw moving particles of light that flowed continuously, unendingly, everlastingly through the landscape, the world, perhaps even the Universe itself. God particles, the Librarian had once said. I didn't know what to call them, but to my eyes, they were alive and moving, and they lit the world up for me, even on the darkest of nights, or in the darkest of rooms.

Or in the darkest of forests.

The wolf and I covered a lot of ground. Unlike when I summoned my winged friend Talos, Kingsley actually turned into a real wolf. A true shape-shifter. And it was often a painful process, but the more he did it, the more muscle—and bone—memory he had, so to speak. Which would explain why the wolf following behind me was so honkin' big. After all, it was Kingsley's muscles and tissues and bones that made up the wolf. Just as his own flesh and blood made up the hulking, two-legged wolfman he became each full moon. Wolf and wolfman were two different shapes. One, he could do at will, the other was forced upon him by his own inner demon.

At a level clearing, we paused, and the wolf brushed up against me, his shoulders as high as my hips. Neither of us were breathing hard. Both of our heads were on swivels. We were now high above the road. In the far distance, I could see faintly flashing lights, and even picked up sirens and voices.

Kingsley probably heard and saw a lot more, although how much he comprehended in his wolf form, even he didn't know. According to him, the whole experience was only a vague, dream-like memory. Apparently, his human mind shut off, and something animalistic and wild took over. He had only vague memories of running free, of speed and strength, of agility and stamina. Back in human form, the memories were mostly lost to him.

So, for all intents and purposes, Kingsley was gone and there was a real wolf standing next to me. A thickly-muscled wolf with wide triangular ears that could probably hear a snoring field mouse, if field mice indeed snored. His sloped back ended in a tail that rarely, if ever, wagged. Twin blasts of superheated steam jetted from his nostrils, billowing out into the cold night. His eyes flashed amber within all that darkness and they glanced at me now.

I cautiously rested a hand on his wide head, and felt the strength of the creature. It radiated up from him and into me, and, seemed, somehow, to give me more strength. He leaned into me, and seemed to like my touch.

As I scanned the cathedral of jagged peaks and ridges around me, I saw the futility of our search. Even running at warp speed, this was too much mountain to cover. So, I did the only thing a girl in my situation could do. That is, a girl who could turn into an honest-to-God dragon.

I disrobed quickly, rolling and shoving my clothing into the small backpack I'd been sporting. Now, naked and feeling the chill, and with a pair of amber eyes intent on me, I climbed the nearest pile of boulders, with which this mountain was littered.

"Find him, Kingsley," I said.

The wolf cocked his head to one side. Did his wolfie self even understand English? Did he understand that we were, in fact, looking for a lost boy? I think the creature understood exactly what I was saying. It just didn't know what the hell I was doing on the rocks.

I grinned at the simple Kingsley before me, the powerful and free Kingsley, and summoned the single flame. I held it in my mind's eye, and saw the creature within it. A creature from mythology, a creature that put the "bad" and "ass" in badass.

Then I leaped as high as I could from the boulders. I briefly caught sight of the wolf shying away, retreating into the shadows, before bounding up another trail, moving as swiftly as anything on this planet.

That is, anything without wings.

The transformation was instant, and now I flapped mine, hard, and found enough lift to clear the closest evergreens, although their turgid spires grazed my belly. Somehow, I managed not to giggle.

I thrust my powerful, thickly membraned wings down, creating so much force and lift that I was soon rocketing up into the sky.

Higher and higher.

Chapter Eleven

Wings outstretched, I glided in a slow, concentric circle, using Talos's eagle-like eyes to see deep into the mountain passes and gorges.

I prefer "dragon-like," came his words.

My bad, I thought.

Not far from here, perhaps thirty miles away, I had broken up a blood sport of sorts. A gang of local werewolves, who preferred their food fresh and with a racing pulse, were unlike my disgusting boyfriend who had a taste for the rotten and the putrid. Unfortunately for the local werewolves, their "food" had been the wife of a local sheriff deputy I'd befriended. I say unfortunately, because every last one of them was dead now. Of course, I'd had some help...

I caught an updraft of surprisingly warm air, and I allowed it to lift me. Talos's wings undulated and absorbed and adjusted, and I loved every moment of every second that I was up here, in the heavens, seeing what I was seeing, feeling what I was feeling.

Would feel even better, I thought, *if I found the boy.*

I saw the various search parties far below, and I stayed above the helicopter. I even spied my own friends, moving in twos along the mountainside, flashlight beams strafing the ground. I saw hundreds, if not thousands, of smaller and not so small pairs of bright spots: raccoons and rodents, skunks and deer. All lit brightly for my eyes only.

When I take on Talos's form, I take on his obvious physical attributes. Interestingly, I retain some of my own. One of which is my own unique night vision, which, when combined with Talos's ultra-powerful eyes, formed quite a one-two punch.

Do you have your own night vision, Talos? I asked, as we continued our search, gliding high enough to avoid being spotted by the search parties, but not so high that I couldn't spot a small, smoldering fire in a shallow cave.

I do have night vision, Sam, but it's not quite as pervasive as your own.

I help you see better into the night?

You do, Sam.

So that would mean I am kind of awesome?

Very, very awesome. And maybe a little needy.

I would have grinned, except Talos's thick dragon lips didn't do much in the way of expressing. I would have laughed, too, except Talos's laughter sounded more like a guttural roar that scared even me.

And you think the short, sharp, barks of

laughter from you humans are easy on the ears? You squeaky things.

Now, I did laugh, despite myself, and the sound came out a little louder than I expected. And a little brighter too, as a spark of fire shot out of my mouth, sizzling and smoking, until it disappeared.

Oops, I thought. *I sparked.*

I sensed Talos's own laughter deep inside my mind, as I angled toward a promising nearby canyon, a canyon that seemed to be within hiking distance, even for a seven-year-old boy.

***

It had not yet been reached by searchers, although some rescuers were working in this direction.

Now that I was away from the helicopter, I flew a little lower. Anyone looking up would have been hard-pressed to see me at all, unless they occasionally spotted the dragon-shaped shadow crossing between them and the stars.

I dropped even lower, and angled toward an outcropping of boulders piled at the bottom of a steep cliff. For the boy to have reached this place, he would have had to hike all evening, through fairly rugged terrain, all while not wearing nearly enough warm clothing.

I could not imagine the boy going much further than this, outside of being picked up by someone. Still, much of this terrain was steep. Even an all-terrain vehicle would have had problems. Hell, a horse might even have problems.

No, I thought. The kiddo had hoofed it on foot, and if my judgment was right, no boy could have hiked further than this, not in the time allowed. I'd already scanned closer locations, many of which were being swarmed over, even now, by local search and rescue.

My location was at the far edge, the perimeter, of a small boy's capabilities.

This area felt right.

This stack of boulders felt right, too.

This wasn't a psychic hit. At least, I didn't think it was. Besides, I didn't get much, if any, such hits. This was an intuitive hit. The kind of hit I'd always received back in the good old days, back when I worked for the federal government and was married to a new attorney named Danny Moon. Or, more precisely, back before I became a creature of the night. Then again, I'd recently learned that I'd been a witch down through the ages, through my many incarnations.

Long story short, I might have more of a sixth sense than I'd previously realized. Was it too late to cultivate it? I didn't know.

But what I did know was that a small glow about midway up the pile of boulders seemed promising.

Very, very promising.

Chapter Twelve

After shifting back to my spunky human self, I dug into the backpack Talos had been lugging around for me, dressed quickly, and checked my cell phone. A handful of messages from the others, mostly checking in and reporting no leads. Mostly, I was impressed with the cell service up here.

Sporting Asics, jeans, and a tee-shirt (along with a pair of my sweats/pajamas, my light jacket, and an extra pair of thick socks shoved in my backpack, along with a handful of granola bars I'd swiped from the cabin's pantry), I scrambled rapidly up the stack of boulders. Like a dang spider.

If ever there was a heap of boulders under which a colony of rattlesnakes lived, this was it. I was seriously going to freak out if I saw a snake. I didn't, thank God. At least, not yet.

I climbed toward the small flickering glow.

The kid had picked a helluva place to hunker down—that is, of course, if this flickering glow was indeed him... and if he was still alive.

A grim thought, for sure. I nearly paused and scanned ahead, as I'm sometimes wont to do, but I decided against it. Hell, I was almost to the glowing mouth of the cave. I would discover who or what was in there... in real time.

Chapter Thirteen

"Halt!" said a child's voice.

I was just scrambling up onto the lip of the cave, and was just about to get my first view into the glowing cave, when I spied a pair of dirty sneakers and dirty socks encrusted with cockleburs—and the unwavering point of a wooden sword. Pointed, mind you, at my face.

"I'm halting," I said.

"Who goes there?"

"I, Samantha Moon, goes there. Or here."

The little sneakers took a step or two closer. I saw some mosquito bites on the calves. Both knees were skinned and I could smell a little boy. I knew because I had one of those at home, a boy who got dirty and was hard on his body.

The bitch inside of me rose up, interested in the small boy's bloodied knees. I quelled her with a silent, *Don't even think about it, bitch!*

The point of the sword was now inches from my face.

"State your business," said the little voice. Little, but firm. "Now." Little, but fearless.

The sword had been sharpened recently, perhaps by rubbing it against a nearby rock's surface. It could have been something a child would make with his dad. The cross guard was even and centered correctly. There was a chance the sword could have been purchased in a pirate gift shop, too. The knuckles holding it were freshly skinned. The little guy had had a tough time of it today.

Now, for the first time, I looked past the sword and scraped knuckles, past the dirt-smudged arm and torn sleeve, all the way up to the little boy staring down at me. It was, of course, the same little boy I had seen earlier. Same clothing. Same thin tee-shirt. Same shock of red hair. What I hadn't seen at the time, or hadn't been close enough to see, were his eyes. They were determined eyes, bold eyes, captivating eyes. His aura, which hovered around him like an angelic glow, was pure and golden and streaked with blues and greens. No mark of the silver dragon, I noted. I'd almost half-expected to see one.

Then I looked past him at the fire in the cave, at the small rock he was using as a seat, and at the paperback Rick Riordan novel about gods and Olympians. Impressive reading for one so young. And, he had a flashlight for reading it. I noted the can of Coke and the half-eaten sandwich still resting on a plastic baggie. Obviously, I had disturbed his dinner. One thing was very, very obvious.

The boy was not lost. *Not in the least.*

Hell, he was less lost than I was.

"I am here to seek warmth from the cold," I said, bowing slightly.

The sword wavered for the first time, then dropped to the rocky cave opening.

"Very well, Samantha Moon, you may seek warmth with me, in my cave."

"Um, thank you," I said, and pulled myself all the way up and stood for the first time in the small shelter.

The boy turned his back to me and rummaged deeper in the cave, itself lit brightly from the fire crackling in the center. The boy, who had holstered his sword in his shorts' belt loops, now lugged a big twenty-pound rock next to the fire, opposite his. He turned back to me.

"Have a seat," he said, pointing. It wasn't a question. And, yes, he took this all very seriously.

I was getting to the point where my own relief needed release, along with seeing so much cuteness in one pint-sized package that I wanted to burst. But I held it together, though, hard as it was to do. Before I sat, I might have dusted off the rock a bit. This was, after all, a civilized cave shelter.

So, I kept a straight face as the solemn-looking boy sat across from me, the tip of his sword resting in the dirt next to him. We both studied each other. His little face, with his tight mouth, dirty round cheeks, and bright eyes, was beyond adorable.

"This is, um, a nice place you've got here."

He nodded once, and might have realized he was taking the whole "ruler of the realm" thing a bit far. "I'm just staying here for now," he said, shrugging and loosening up. "Say, are you hungry? I have another sandwich. It's a PJ and B," he said, mixing up the letters. I might have squeaked at the overload of cuteness.

When the wave of cuteness passed, I nodded and said sure. He reached eagerly into a backpack I had missed seeing, back when I'd first seen him dart off the road. He handed me a goopy sandwich, heavy on the jelly. I took out one half, noting it had been cut from corner to corner, and not too carefully. I left him the bigger half.

He reached into his backpack again, and produced another can of Coke. He blew on it, then pulled the tab for me. The hiss echoed in the small enclosure. He handed it to me with, I swear to God, a small bow.

"Thank you, good sir," I said.

He smiled and nearly bowed again, then returned to his rock, and we both produced chewing and slurping sounds. I hadn't yet taken my eyes off him. There were no indications that he had been physically abused, although it was hard to tell with all the scrapes and smudges he'd acquired on his evening jaunt on his walkabout.

Was he a runway? I ventured a guess. "Do you live here?"

He smiled, then laughed, then slapped his knee and giggled nearly uncontrollably. I was suddenly reminded of Anthony, and now, I really, really loved this little boy. "No, no, no, Samantha Moon. This is just my camp for the night."

"I see," I said, although I was still far from seeing. "And how many nights do you, ah, plan on staying here?"

"Just one night." He giggled. "I only brought two sandwiches!"

"Silly me. Do your parents know you're gone?"

He nodded vigorously. "I left them a note."

"A handwritten note?"

"Yes, silly. I'm too young to text."

"Where did you leave the note?"

And just as I asked the question, as a big glob of jelly landed on the cave floor between my feet, I said, "You taped it on the jar of jelly."

"Close! On the peanut butter. Right on top so no one would miss it. Daddy eats peanut butter, like, all the time."

I tapped my head. "Smart," I said to him.

Except, of course, Daddy probably only ate peanut butter in the morning. Flynn beamed and ate, and the fire crackled. I asked him where he'd learned to build a fire and he said he was studying YouTube videos and, besides, it wasn't that hard if you had dry tinder and kindling. He reached into his backpack and pulled out, from separate zippered pockets, a piece of steel wool and a 9-volt battery.

"If you touch them together with the top thingies on the battery, the steel wool catches on fire." He put away the items carefully in separate pockets of his backpack. "And you have to have a place for the smoke to go away."

He looked up and I did, too, and saw the starry night—a whistling hole in the cave ceiling, right above where he'd built his fire.

Smart kid.

I finished my half-sandwich and told him I was full. He wanted me to keep it, and so I stuffed it in my own backpack, oddly warmed by his generosity. Like the kid had said, he only had the two sandwiches. Although, Lord only knew how many cans of Coke were in there.

I asked for his name, although I already knew it, except I didn't want to let on that I knew it. He gave me his complete name, middle name and all, and it was all I could do to not giggle at that, too.

"Here's the million-dollar question, Flynn," I asked, after he added another stick to the crackling fire, doing so very seriously and studiously, the light reflecting in his big green eyes.

He looked up at from across the fire. "Yes?"

"Why are you camping here, in the woods, all alone?"

He looked out the cave opening, which was behind me. We were high up and the opening afforded a view of the stars and crescent moon, and distant peaks and faraway places.

"I want to be an explorer," he said. "I want to discover new things. I want to see new things. I don't want anyone or anything to ever stop me from exploring."

"I know what you mean about people stopping you from doing things. Boy, do I know. So, do you plan on spending the night in here?"

"Yes."

"Do you often spend the night in caves, alone?"

"No. This is my first time."

"Are you afraid?"

He looked at me, his green eyes flashing. "I'm not afraid of anything."

I shook my head and nearly whistled, because I believed every word that came from him. As I thought about his words, he asked if he could show me something. I said sure.

While he dug into his backpack, I sent a quick group text to my team. "Found him, safe and sound. We are camping in a cave. Call the sheriff. Call the mom."

He produced, of all things, a *National Geographic* magazine. Flynn flipped through the magazine, as my silenced phone lit up like a Christmas tree for the next few minutes, as the desperate and eager messages came pouring in. I ignored it as the little guy showed me an article about his favorite adventurer, an Englishman named Henry Worsley, who'd spent his life exploring and setting records, a man who had tragically died only thirty miles from completing the first-ever solo Antarctic trek.

"He was a very famous explorer," I said.

"I know it. I looked at his Facebook page and blog almost every day."

"You're on Facebook?" I thought he was too young for that.

"My dad lets me. My mom doesn't."

That, I understood.

"Are you sad that he died?" I asked. "Your explorer?"

He looked away, his eyes suddenly gleaming. "He was only thirty miles from finishing."

"I see that. Do you think he was brave?"

"The bravest ever."

"And you want to be like him?"

"Yes."

"Is that why you came out here tonight, to honor his memory?"

I expected him to shrug, or to not really understand my question. He was only seven, after all. But his eyes met mine with a strength that was palpable.

"Yes. Honor is a good word."

"Is that why you didn't wear a jacket?" I asked. "Or long pants?"

"No," he said. "I just forgot. But I won't, next time."

"Next time?" I grinned and reached out and roughed-up his tangle of thick hair, and he giggled a little.

We sat back on our rocks and I found myself thinking of the English explorer, now passed away, who had inspired a little boy he'd never met—and, no doubt, inspired little boys and girls around the world—to do the bravest thing this little boy could think of, which was to spend the night, alone, in a cave. Worsley was a true hero. It also occurred to me that even great explorers were once little boys. As I looked across the fire at the determined little guy who was staring bravely into it, I could not imagine

anyone or anything stopping him.
   Ever.

Chapter Fourteen

It was later.

Detective Sherbet had passed along a message from Flynn's mother, who desperately wanted to see her boy. So, I'd sent her a selfie of Flynn and me drinking our Cokes, next to the fire. She had asked me to bring him down, immediately. But I'd told her that I couldn't do that, that her son was honoring the name of a fallen explorer. I also said that we needed daylight to make a safe descent down the mountain. That was certainly true, especially since I didn't plan on breaking out my wings in front of Flynn. Not anytime soon.

Ten minutes later, her response had come back, via Sherbet: she understood. Her son, she stated, was a brave little boy, and she would see us in the morning.

According to Knighthorse, the search was called off. The team all asked if they could crash at the cabin, and I thanked them from the bottom of my heart and told them, *mi casa es su casa*. Knighthorse replied that he didn't speak Spanish and he would get Sanchez to translate. And since this was a group text, Sanchez immediately wrote back: *Fuck off, Knighthorse.*

With the team hunkered down at the cabin,

and the search called off, Flynn and I spent time gathering more branches for the fire from his pile and snapping them into smaller pieces. We had just gotten that sucker roaring when Flynn, looking out the cave opening, and suddenly gasped.

I turned and looked and saw a massive shadow appearing from over the lip of the cave, a shadow that took the form of a wolf.

A big, black, hairy wolf.

With amber eyes.

Chapter Fifteen

I nearly leapt up and moved between wolf and boy, but something strange was happening.

Although Flynn had initially gasped, he didn't run or back away, or show any fear. He was that intrepid. That fearless. That curious. I had no doubt that someday, he was going to make one hell of an explorer.

How much of Kingsley was here, I didn't know. I suspected that the longer he was in wolf form, the more he forgot his human nature. In fact, the creature before us may very well have been all wolf.

After all, its hackles were up, and a low growl emanated from its massive chest.

Again, I nearly stood and shielded the boy and commanded the wolf to leave, if he would even listen to me. But, again, I stayed put on my rock. Never had the wolf looked so big as it did now, filling the opening. Our only exit. Blocked.

A musty, dirty, earthy, bloody scent reached my nostrils, and I realized that Kingsley had feasted tonight. Or the wolf had. Well, at least he probably had a full belly. Certainly, he had rolled in something dead. *Long dead.*

Flynn rose slowly, from where he sat at the

back end of the shallow cave. And then, he did something that I didn't think I ever could have expected. I mean, *ever.*

He approached the wolf, hand held out, palm up, as if he were approaching a neighbor's dog and offering a nonthreatening place to sniff. As he did so, I watched the boy's eyes, and detected nothing but excitement. Nothing but curiosity. No fear. No hesitation. Hell, *joy.*

The wolf continued its low, guttural growl. No, not a growl. It began as a deep, low-frequency roar that began in his chest and vibrated out through his flaring nostrils. This throaty, roaring, snorting snarl was both awesome and frightening. And there was saliva dripping. Lots of it.

"It's okay, boy," said Flynn, now moving around the fire, and when I saw what the boy was doing, tears sprang instantly to my eyes. Flynn was moving between me and the wolf. Flynn was protecting *me.*

I turned on my rock, watching all of this play out, also aware that even heroes were once little boys, too.

"It'll be okay, Samantha," said Flynn. "I'll protect you."

"I know you will, sweetie."

He turned his face toward me, although he didn't take his eyes off the black wolf. "I'm not a sweetie. I'm an explorer."

"Oops, right. Sorry."

I dashed away my tears with the back of my hand.

He nodded, satisfied, and turned his full attention to the wolf standing in the cave entrance, a wolf that, even now, seemed like it was oh-so-close to pouncing. Kingsley was in there, somewhere, and he would win out. He had to.

Flynn continued holding out his hand, continued creeping closer, and the black wolf's growl deepened, seemingly vibrating the very rock I was sitting on. But still the boy inched forward.

The growling was heinous enough to make the hairs rise on the back of my own neck. A primitive reaction. "Flynn, be careful." Yeah, that was the momma in me.

"It's okay," he said. "We're all friends here. Aren't we, fella?"

Kingsley dropped his head, and turned it from side to side, showing the boy his extremely long teeth. Teeth that had never seen a toothbrush. Teeth that had tatters of fur and rotted flesh hanging from them. Unlike Kingsley's magazine-perfect white smile.

"You're a big doggie. Are you hungry? I have some of my sandwich left. Samantha might give you some of hers, too."

He huffed at us. The wolf's breath was... putrid. Out of politeness, I held back a gag.

And still Flynn stood his ground.

Boy stood directly before wolf.

I could hear both heartbeats. The boy's, a rapid *tap-tap* of adrenaline-fueled excitement. The wolf's heartbeat, a slower, deeper *thump-thump*. I had no idea what the wolf was thinking. Or why my hearing was suddenly so acute.

"I'm your friend," Flynn said to the wolf. "We both are."

Outside, the wind whistled past the cave opening, bringing with it the myriad scents of a fully functioning and active forest: pine needles, decomposing logs, tree fungi, acorns. The wolf's fur shuddered in the wind, lifting and falling, and now, finally, the creature eased forward one step, then another, on those silent, massive paws. The wolf sniffed the proffered grubby hand. And his wolf lips relaxed downward to cover the long teeth.

I breathed a sigh of relief, even though I hadn't realized I was holding my breath.

As the wolf loudly snuffled the little hand, Flynn looked back and shot me a wink, although he mostly blinked both eyes, not really knowing how to wink.

Now the wolf was gently licking Flynn's

hand with its long, dark-pink tongue. Correction, the wolf was licking the peanut butter off his hand, all while Flynn giggled and patted its wide, flat head with his free, non-slobbery hand.

For the first time ever, I witnessed the wolf's tail wag.

Wagging tail? Oh, Kingsley would never, *ever* live this down.

Outside, the wind picked up and distant coyote howls reached even my ears. Kingsley's own perked up, but he mostly ignored the sounds. After all, the little boy now climbing on his back had his full attention as the kiddo found all of the itchy places on the wolf—itchy places he couldn't reach—and gave him a good, old-fashioned scratching. All along his sides. Between the shoulder blades. Behind the ears. Under the chin. That spot on the rump that canines wish they could reach, but really can't. The wolf whined in pleasure at being affectionately roughed up by the small hands of a small explorer.

And then, Flynn threw back his head and began to howl. Yes, howl. And then, it was the darnedest thing: the wolf threw back his head and howled back. Together, they raised their voices in eerie, heartrending cries as old as the ages, and as young as this very moment where a wolf and a human… bonded.

I giggled as goosebumps rose on my arms in response to their soulful wolf song. Which went on for several minutes. They didn't even seem to realize I was here, listening. Spellbound.

I brought my knees up to my chest and wrapped my arms around them until their howling ceased and some roughhousing began. I watched wolf and boy begin to wrestle in the small cave, limbs tangling and bodies tumbling over and over each other, amid lots and lots of tail wagging and slobbering and laughter. And I found, in those precious moments, magic—the 'rarest kind of magic' that Kingsley had promised me for this Valentine weekend. It was not kid-free, vampire-free or werewolf-free magic. It was simply… *magic*.

While the fire crackled and the wind whistled, the outside world, the real world, seemed only a distant, fading memory.

The End

Moon Musings

Author's Notes: Moon Musings

Years ago, back when I was on a blog tour to promote my latest Samantha Moon novel, I wrote a "character blog." That is, a blog written by my main character, Sam Moon. It was a short blog (a single page), and I quite enjoyed writing it (in fact, it's being published here as "Blog Post #1"). So, a few years ago, after writing *Moon Angel* (book #14), I revisited the blog idea, and wrote three more in Sam's voice. I never knew what to do with them, and left them sitting on my computer; that is, until I decided to collect the blog posts in this little anthology of revealing Sam Moon short stories. So, want to know what a vampire might blog about? Read on... and I do hope you enjoy!

~~~~~

Blog Post #1

Some call me a vampire.

I say, why use labels? I'm uncomfortable calling myself anything other than a mother. That's the one label I am comfortable with. I'm a mom first and foremost. A private investigator next, even though that is fairly recent. Seven years ago, I wasn't a private eye, but a federal agent.

So, even that was subject to change. Perhaps someday I might find myself better suited for a different job, although I will always help those who need help. Although I'd always admired Judge Judy, I would never want to be in her position: to judge the actions of others. That took wisdom...a lifetime of wisdom. Technically, I'm only in my mid-thirties, although I look much younger. Still, far too young to judge others.

Truth was, my current lifestyle was perfectly suited to private investigation. Other than meeting new clients, who tended to want to meet during the day, I got along just fine working the night shift.

So, yes, one of the constants in my life was that I was a mother. Of course, even that was threatened just a year or so ago, when a rare sickness almost took my son from me. A son who was growing so fast.

Supernaturally fast.

Don't ask.

I have a daughter, too. A daughter who offered many challenges, the least of which was that she could read minds as easily as she read her Facebook newsfeed.

Yes, I was a mother...and a sister. My sister has had a rough time of it, of late. She's recently been introduced to some of the darker elements of my world, and might be holding a grudge against me. But she would get over it. She's better. I need her in my life.

Of course, there was another constant in my life...a constant that I ignored. A constant that I denied. And, as they say, denial isn't just a river in Egypt.

Denial is my sanity.

You see, I have to deny what I am. Who I am. Or I would go crazy. I know I would. In fact, a part of me is certain that I just might be crazy. But let's not go there.

Yes, call me anything. But please, just please, don't call me a vampire.

At least, not to my face.

Blog Post #2

Let's try this again:
My name is Samantha, and I'm a vampire.
I am also a mother, a sister, a friend, a divorcee, and a private investigator. I am a taxpayer. I am an entrepreneur. I am a daughter, too. I am many things. I am a college graduate. I am a girlfriend. I am an ex-federal agent. I am many normal, mundane things. I am a reader, a viewer, a listener, a gossip, a prankster, too. I am fun, and sometimes, I am even funny. At least, I think I am. I am interested in the world, but not so interested in politics.

My name is Samantha, and I'm a vampire.
I am also your neighbor, your friend, and your private eye for when you don't know who else to turn to. I am the person in line behind you at the supermarket, the person you cut off in traffic. I am the person who doesn't blink enough, although you might not consciously know it. I am the person who shows up as blurry in the background of your photos. But if you look again, it's not that I'm blurry, it's that I'm missing. Parts of me, anyway.

You see, I never show up in digital photographs or on film or in mirrors... unless I'm wearing copious amounts of makeup. And I do, mostly. But sometimes I forget. And those are the days when you might notice the woman in the background of your vacation pics with no ears, or no forehead.

My friend Fang has a theory about that. Yes, Fang. You will learn more about Fang, I'm sure, as these blogs continue. If they continue. We'll take it one blog at a time and see how it goes. In fact, it was Fang who convinced me to start a blog, to share my story with the world, and to even earn extra income.

Let's try this again. My name Samantha and I am a vampire. Yes, I said a vampire. And no, you won't get my last name. In fact, I won't even admit that Samantha is my real name. But it is. Or not. Why am I here? Why am I blogging? Well, I'm still sorting that out.

My friend Fang doesn't think it's a good idea to blog about my life. Yes, his name is Fang. No, it's not his real name. He thinks I might inadvertently give away too many secrets. He thinks I might also attract undue attention. I told him I would be purposefully coy, with little or no clues leading back to me. I also told him I probably won't talk about the creepiest parts of my life, although I do record many of those creepy things in my case notes. I think, deep down, Fang really worries that his *own* secrets might be exposed in my blog. But after all these years, he should really trust me more.

Yes, I have case notes. And yes, I have strange friends, some of whom drink blood. And one other who feasts on carrion. By day, though usually at night, I work as a private eye. I used to work as a federal agent, although I'll refrain from saying which branch (you see, Fang, I can be mysteriously vague). But after my attack eleven years ago, I was forced to quit my day job and work for myself as a private investigator. As one of my cop friends says— he's a homicide detective in my hometown— I'm a private dick with no dick. Guy humor. Insert eye rolls.

No, I won't reveal my own name, and, yes, I will do my best to keep the clues to a minimum so that all of you out there with too much time on your hands can't find me. That's already happened to me once (I'm looking at you, Fang). So, I will purposely leave red herrings and insert diversions. No real names, no real cities.

I'm not trying to be frustrating, but I think most of you would understand my need to keep my anonymity. Of course, I also understand that many of you, if not all of you, will believe this blog to be a farce, perhaps a gimmick of some sort, to bring in advertising revenue. Although the advertising revenue is appealing (and it's one of the top three reasons why I'm doing this), I'm certainly not doing this just for the money, nor am I under any delusion that I will make a great deal of money. How much ad money can a WordPress blog generate, anyway? I don't know, but if it can pay my cable bill each month, I'm game. (Maybe Netflix and Hulu, too.)

Truthfully, I like thinking I have an outlet. I like thinking that I don't have to keep all of this inside me. Yes, I do have friends—some very good friends who will remain nameless. Okay, I'll name one: Allison. (Sorry, Allie.) And yes, my friends and family have provided that outlet I need, but it's just not enough. Living with secrets is hell. Living with many dozens of secrets is exponentially hellish. Having one's whole life be one big ass secret is a burden I wouldn't wish on my worst enemy. Then again, all of my worst enemies share nearly the same secret. So, I guess we're all in this mess together. The good, the bad, and the really ugly.

So, welcome to my blog. Welcome to my life. My name is Samantha and I might be your neighbor, I might be your friend, and I might have looked at you a little too long for your comfort. And if you were uncomfortable, there's a very good chance I might have simply removed your memory of me. I can do that, you see. I can get inside your head and mess with your memories. I can remove them or suppress them. Oh, and I can know your secrets, too. And if you hang around me too long, you will know my secrets, as well. If I get to know you a little too well, we unconsciously form a sort of mind link. Also, some of me spills over into you. It all happens quite by accident and it has caused me untold embarrassment.

If you were really, really observant, you might notice that my sharp nails aren't just a fad. Look a little more closely and you will see that my nails aren't just sharp, but grotesquely thick, too. God, I hate my nails. Honestly, I could live with just about any part of vampirism, but my thick, sharp, gross nails just might be the hardest part to deal with.

Why do I care about my nails? Good question. I'm sure some vampires don't care. In fact, I would even hazard to say, most don't care. Then again, not all vampires have such nails. Some have normal nails. You see, not all vampires are created equally. This came as a bit of a surprise to me. Turns out, there's only a handful of universal rules for vampires. Yes, most shy away from the sun. Yes, most drink blood. As far as universals rules go, that's it.

Everything else varies. Some vampires can

turn into giant dragon-like creatures (guilty). Some vampires can read minds (guilty again). Some vampires can see into the future (barely guilty; it's only happened twice, and only during lucid dreaming). Some vampires can't stand water (not me, I love hot showers, the hotter the better). Some vampires never blink or breathe (guilty and guilty). Some have a heartbeat, and some don't (I do, but barely). Some vampires cannot only read minds, but also take control of a mind. (I've never taken control, but I have certainly given many 'suggestions.') Some vampires can erase memories (guilty as charged). Most vampires prefer the blood of living humans. Truthfully, I do, too. But consuming such blood presents problems. Let me explain.

You see, something lives inside me. And that something is sort of the reason why we're even here. That something is called a highly evolved dark master. You've heard of Buddhist masters? Enlightened holy men? Think the opposite, and you will be on the right track. And, yeah, one of these bastards—or, in my case, bitches—lives inside of me. From now until eternity. Or until I die, which can happen, despite my 'immortal' label. Yes, something lives inside of me, something dark and nasty and angry and hungry and powerful and controlling, and it is *she* who craves the fresh blood of humans. Which is why I do all I can to never, ever give her what she really wants.

And drinking fresh blood straight from a victim's vein is exactly what she wants. Why? Because it makes her stronger. Granted, it makes me stronger, too. But I never, ever want her so strong that she can take over my body. You see, the thing within me, whose name may or may not be Elizabeth (I'm being coy again), wants nothing more than to take over me completely, and use me to help bring back all of her banished brothers and sisters, but that is another story for another day. Or another blog.

Speaking of another story, I have a doozy for you, but I think it might be beyond the scope and breadth of this blog. And what is the scope and breadth of this blog? I don't know yet, exactly, but trust me, any story that involves the devil, his three-headed dog, and the Angel of Death himself, is well beyond a friendly blog.

Then again, I don't know how friendly this blog will be. To many of you, it will seem like the rantings of a crazy person. To many more, you will see this as fiction. But to a few of you it will have the ring of truth. Oh, yes, this blog will thrill—and chill—some of you to the bone.

Then again, many of you believe, and you should believe, for I am real, and we are real, and despite how much I tried to deny it, ignore it, or even call it something else (a medical condition, in fact), there is no denying what I am--and what I became eleven years ago. A lifetime ago, really. Who could imagine so much could change in eleven years? But it has, and it continues changing, evolving, growing into something beyond my wildest dreams.

Okay, I'm back. I had to pause and make dinner for my son. My daughter is... indisposed at the moment. To where, I would rather not say. Okay, fine. I'll say. She's spending time with a man I call the Librarian. Sometimes I call him the Alchemist because he is both. He is another immortal, but he is not possessed like the rest of us. No, his immortality is gained through potions and elixirs and precisely worded incantations that take hours each day. How he does this, day after day, month after month, year after year, I do not know. But I suppose it beats death. Certainly it beats my own death, since there's no coming back for me. I will literally meet my maker. I'll just leave it at that.

So here I am, blogging my ass off. Yes, I have some work to do, but the sun hasn't set and I'm not up to doing any more than sitting here and watching my fingers fly over the keyboard. Truth be known, I'm finding this therapeutic.

I'm sure Allison will tease me to no end about it. No doubt, she'll criticize my writing skills, or lack thereof. Little does she know that I write up many of the cases I work on and save them in a secret safe. Shh, don't tell her. That may or may not be true. Sometimes, I think of myself as the "vampire for hire." Silly, I know, but, in reality, that's exactly what I am.

Yes, I've written up each of my more interesting cases. Trust me, not all of them deserve a write-up. But when something strikes me as life-changing or particularly strange, I can often be found in my office, detailing my case, my thoughts, even my conversations. No, I do not see that as writing, per se, and I certainly wouldn't call myself a writer. But I do enjoy the late nights I spend writing up the cases, and then carefully locking them in a safe beneath my office floorboards. There's not much in the safe, just my case notes, a few handguns, and some emergency cash.

Fun fact: I've met God a few times. The last time had been through an automatic writing technique that had segued into a vision of epic proportions. There's a chance—a very good chance—that I had a glimpse of heaven.

And, friends, let me tell you, I can't stop thinking about it. It's beautiful. You will love it. I promise. It's just that, you see, it's not for me.

Or others like me. I'd learned that most human souls are split between heaven and earth, with most of it residing in the world of the energetic. Unless one isn't human. Unless one's humanity has been stolen from them.

I won't bore you with the details, but, immortality is a simple thing, really. Immortality is all of one's soul contained within the physical body. I learned that our souls are immeasurably powerful, for each is a sliver of the Origin or Creator himself (or herself, or itself). Heady stuff. But it all boils down to this: with my soul having been ejected from heaven, there is no going back. Once removed, always removed.

Of course, on the plus side, having my soul fully contained in my physical body has its advantages, and many of them I am only just exploring. The downside is, despite the immortal label, I can still be killed. What happens then is something I would rather not think about. No, I don't cease to exist, but I might as well. Being re-absorbed into God doesn't sound very appealing, although God made it sound like a hoot. Myself, I wasn't so sure.

You see, I like being autonomous. I like being a free thinking creature. I like loving and being loved. And I like watching my life continue to expand and grow. I especially like watching my kids grow. I doubt I would be aware of any of that once I'm re-absorbed into God, which, quite frankly, just sounds terrible.

Then again, I have no plans of dying anytime soon, if ever. I haven't asked for this lot in life, but here it is, and I am going to make the best of it. And make the most of it.

Don't feel too badly for me. I still have my kids, although the devil did his best to see to it that I almost didn't. Yes, the devil. Definitely a story for another time. And Tammy still may not be out of the woods. Which is why she's working closely with the Librarian. I think she will be fine. I hope she will be fine. God, what would I do without her? No, no, she will be fine. I have to believe it. Besides, she's in good hands now.

Blog Post #3

Back again.

Just took a call from a potential new client. I use the word "potential" loosely here. I think he wanted someone to unload on, someone who would agree with him that his wife is a no-good cheating whore. And then he started crying. Unfortunately, my telepathic connection reaches only so far, and so I could only sit here, in my home office, and listen to him blubber on the other end. Otherwise, I would have prompted him to get to the point, although I would never have prompted him to give me his money, or to hire me unnecessarily.

Anyway, when he'd finally gotten hold of himself—and when I was well into a new game of Spider Solitaire (on mute, of course), he had asked what I had thought. I hadn't, of course, been listening. I get at least one such call a day, maybe even two or three, and they are all the same. Little-known fact about private eyes: we've heard it all. There's nothing you can say that we haven't heard. There's nothing that will shock us or horrify us. We've heard every cheating angle possible, and it bores us to no end. We take the work because we have to. Most of us—nay, all of us—need the money.

There, I said it. And, yes, I wrote 'nay' for the first time in my life.

Anyway, when the poor sap was done pouring out his heart, I gave him my standard spiel. I told him that most people who come to a private eye already know their spouses are cheating, but we can provide solid proof, if that's necessary. Some need it to help win a divorce settlement. Some just won't believe it until they see it, despite evidence to the contrary. As a private eye, I can follow cheaters and photograph them legally. A private citizen cannot. A good private eye can catch the adulterer in the act. A private citizen would probably screw it up. A good private eye has all the correct equipment to gather the evidence. Evidence is crucial in cases where alimony is at stake. Proving an affair goes a long way in court, even in a no-fault divorce state.

I take this kind of work because I need it, but usually, it's a dirty business and I'm not proud of what I do. But I have been cheated on, and it's a terrible feeling. Perhaps even one of the worst, and if I can help some people uncover the truth and move on with their lives, well, then I can at least live with myself.

Anyway, once I quoted him my weekly rate, which is what I charge for any cheating spouse case, he nearly choked. The choking sound is always dismaying. It means I will likely not get hired, and that I just wasted another half hour of my life listening to the sob story and explaining the process. Then again, for someone who may or may not be immortal, what's another half hour, right? At any rate, he hung up soon after, promising he would call when he was ready to hire me, but I knew he was just going to keep calling around until he found a cheaper rate.

So, why do I say "may or may not" be immortal? Well, I've only been at this vampire game for eleven years. Hard to know if you are immortal in eleven years, right? I mean, for all I know, I could be aging gracefully... and slowly. Except I am told that I look as young as I was the day I was attacked, perhaps even a few years younger. Staying out of the sun really does wonders for a body. And having one's soul entirely and completely contained in one's body gives one a healthy glow, too.

Then again, maybe there's something to this blood diet. I drink a hella amount of blood. I usually need it every other day, but I can go as much as four days without it, although that's the limit and by then, look out. I literally might eat your baby. I'm kidding of course. I think.

So, anyway, am I immortal? I guess time will literally tell. I was 31 when I was attacked and rendered into what I am now. So, yeah, from what I hear of people, and from what I can make out through all the makeup I wear, I am often asked if I am in my late twenties. Nothing wrong with that, I guess.

My real age? 42. My sister, who shall remain nameless (okay, let's call her ML), is now 48. Forty-freakin-eight. She's not happy that I look twenty-seven and she looks, well, in her late forties. I tell her she doesn't look a day over thirty-eight. The truth is—and thank God she can't read my mind (no one in my family can, except for my freak of a daughter)—she very much looks her age, perhaps even a tad older, too. I'll never tell her that, and I know ML has taken extreme measures to look younger (facial peels, experimental medicines), but she's losing this battle, and I feel terrible. I know her motivation is me, whether or not she admits it. It's hard for ML to have a sister who's six years younger, but looks nearly twenty years younger. Already, I have heard whispering in my family that there's something a little off about me. Which is why I do not have much of a relationship with my parents. ML is different—we have always been close, and eleven years ago, I told her about the change inside me almost immediately. To her credit, she has done a heckuva job keeping it a secret, although she had let it slip once and now her hubby knows, too. Luckily, her hubby wasn't a blood relation and I had long since given him the vampire suggestion to forget what he'd heard.

Then again, these could be the ramblings of a crazy woman with nothing better to do than scare you, shock you, entertain you, or give you a good laugh. For all I know, these blogs will be read precisely by no one. Maybe they will be blown off and laughed at. And maybe they *should* be blown off and laughed at. Maybe it's better that you don't believe. Maybe it's better —and easier—if I just delete this whole file and *not* hit "publish."

Maybe, but I dunno, I kind of like writing this blog. It has been therapeutic already. I find telling my story oddly calming, and I need some calmness after these past three or four months. I understand why writers write. It's pretty damn relaxing. Yes, writing these words has been challenging. I'm not a natural writer. But seeing these words appear before me now is having a transforming effect on me already. Unlike my copious case notes that I keep hidden, notes that are meant for my eyes only, I just might publish these words, and I find that exhilarating to say the least. I also find it frightening. Will I say too much? Have I already said too much? Do I even care if I have said too much? I don't know yet...

I do want to be careful. Yes, my own enemies might read these words. It may not be prudent to, say, give away my weaknesses, or discuss all of my strengths, or even, quite frankly, go into too much detail about who and what is inside of me.

I do know that keeping names and locations a secret is wise, although I will drop one name: Dracula. Yes, he's real, and, yes, I have met him, more than once. He's not very different than me, and that could be because the entities possessing us were once lovers themselves. Both entities had similar powers. As such, these powers manifest in us in similar ways. For instance, we both can summon something big and powerful and not of this world. Oh, and winged. That's all I'm going to say. Okay fine, one more: think *fire-breathing*.

Okay, now I know I've said too much. But you don't really believe me, right? You don't really believe that a woman born on this earth, a woman who has, perhaps, been waiting behind you at a red light just earlier today, could shape-shift into something not of this world, something winged and fire-breathing?

Of course, you don't. This is just a silly, anonymous blog. Right?

Obviously, I'm not a real vampire.

Obviously, I didn't just drink from a packet

of cow and pig blood just a few hours ago.

Obviously, I didn't have a very pleasant evening with my werewolf boyfriend who also just so happens to be an ace criminal defense attorney. (Okay, I might have said too much there, but let's hope not.)

And obviously, I didn't spend an hour or so on the phone with my witchy friend, listening to her own crazy adventure. My friend can drive me nuts, but I love her. (And I know she's going to read this, and I know she's going to read too much into this, too. Sigh.)

But there are worse problems than being adored by your friends, even if such adoration makes you feel smothered and uncomfortable. I don't make friends easily (I tend to gravitate toward my sister, my boyfriend and work colleagues), but my witchy has made it pretty damn easy to be her friend, even if she's a little pushy and needy. Or a lot pushy and needy. Then again, maybe we all need someone pushy and needy in our lives. Maybe they help us break out of our shell a little.

Side note: The client I mentioned earlier (let's call him Toby), called a few minutes ago. He wants to hire me. I said fine and gave him my PayPal account email address, and, wonder of wonders, the money is there! My son can eat again! And eat and eat and eat. Let's just say he's a growing boy, and leave it at that. Of course, thinking about him makes me automatically think about my daughter. She'll be fine. I know she will. She went through a lot. We all did. But she's gonna be fine. I have to believe that.

Anyway, the client (yes, he's an official client now), also just emailed me back my questionnaire. Sure, I had sent him the questionnaire earlier, with no hope that he would fill it out, let alone send me my $1,000 retainer, but stranger things have happened. Trust me, I know! Or don't trust me. Up to you!

Okay, I'm off to work!

***

Back again. It's nearly five in the morning. What a night. The sun rises in about an hour and trust you me, I will be in bed well before that.

Not too long ago I had vowed to never again take another cheating spouse case. Then a funny thing happened: my mortgage was due. Sigh.

I hope these s don't suck. I did my best. I'm not a writer. I'm just a normal person rendered into something extraordinary. Or something terrible. You pick. Despite the noise of my kids getting ready for school—my daughter now drives them—I'm too sleepy to stay awake for much longer.

My bed and blackout curtains make a soft tomb for rest and reflection. Even though it's spring, I have the blankets piled on me because I am always cold.

Until next time.

Blog Post #4

Hi again!

It's Sam again, your friendly neighborhood vampire who may or may not have eaten your cat. (Sorry about that, by the way.)

Okay, so it's safe to say that my first few blogs were a resounding success. And by success, I mean a middling success. By middling success, I mean a few hundred of you read it. That's a few hundred more than I had before, so I'm pleased. I also spent the last week researching blog ads, and settled on Google Ads. Now, as you might notice, the panels of my blog are filled with mostly Amazon ads that kick you out to various vampire books. I've clicked on one or two myself. As far as I can tell, someone called Bella Forrest seems to have taken over vampire fiction. I'll have to see what the fuss is about.

So what do vampire detectives do during the week? Myself, I prefer to run across graveyards at night, usually in a black flowing robe. I kid, of course. I once heard Anne Rice used to do that with fans on Halloween night. I always thought that sounded fun, although I was never sure of the point of it.

No, I don't run across graveyards, although

my boyfriend just might rob a fresh one, especially if he ever gets out at a full moon, which he doesn't, thanks to his manservant who really is the Frankenstein's monster. Well, one of many. Long story...

Moving on.

Yes, my blog seems to be playing out as I expected it to. Most of you leaving comments find my blog amusing, incorrectly assuming it was fiction. Some of you are pissed off at me (well three of you, and you know who you are) for seeing this as a money grab. Well, if I'm lucky, there might be some money to grab, but I'm really really am here to lighten my load, so to speak. And, yes, I can almost hear my son giggling at that phrase. Indeed, my main purpose is to get all this crap off my chest. Yes, no doubt more snickering from my son. Anyway, I see this blog as my escape valve and even my escape pod out of my own mind. I need an escape. Trust me, you really, really don't want to know what's going on inside my head. It's torture. From keeping the beast within me at bay, to controlling my thoughts about how you might taste (spoiler alert, delicious), to worrying ceaselessly about my kids. Not necessarily in that order. There are days when I am certain that my boyfriend is cheating. He was, after all, a world class player. But I have learned to let that go. I remind myself that I am a helluva catch and that he's lucky to have me, and if he wants to cheat, then he can go ahead and do that. I won't waste another minute worrying about it. Except I do waste many minutes worrying about, but I mostly let it go. After all, there aren't a lot of people like me, and he knows it, and we'll leave it at that.

Besides, I would soon discover that immortals can't have normal relationships with you mortals. Oh? You didn't know that? You've longed to sleep with your favorite vampire hero in your favorite vampire novel? Well, good luck with that. Before you know it, you'll become their love slave. I know, I know, it sounds pretty great. But it's not, trust me. You lose all sense of self, live only to make your immortal happy, even to the detriment of your health, your kids, your life, your dreams. Everything. You don't want that do you? Oh, you do? Sigh. Luckily, your vampire heroes don't really exist, right?

Anyway, I do see two or three comments by some of you who think there is a slim chance I might be telling the truth. I'm looking at you redheart10011. You bring up a good question: can I provide some type of proof that I am a vampire? Let me think on that...

Maybe. We'll see.

Okay, gotta go. I've got a cheating spouse to

catch, and a needy friend to call, and a boyfriend to cook for.

And some blood to drink.
Maybe yours.
I jest, of course.
Until next time.

The End

Moon Memories

Author's Note: Moon Memories

"Moon Memories" is a story in dialogue form; meaning, there is no narration. And no dialogue tags. Because of that, I decided on a single setting, a single scene. I hope you like this change of pace. Final note, the story was started on a tablet computer, and finished on my phone. In a sense, this is one long text crazy text message.

~~~~

"Have a seat."
"Thank you. You work from your home?"
"I do, yes."
"Aren't you worried about bringing riffraff into your home?"
"I did initially. But money was tight. A home office seemed the way to go. If some potential clients seemed a little off, I met them at Starbucks."
"And you could tell they were off just by

talking to them over the phone?"

"That, and running their names in my proprietary database. Oh, and since I had already been a vampire by the time I started my PI business, I used the little warning bell inside my head to let me know if a potential client could be trusted in my home or not. I considered it my advanced asshole warning system."

"Did you say vampire?"

"I did, yes."

"Is that because I can expect to have my bank account sucked dry by the time I'm done hiring you?"

"Cute, but no. I charge fair rates and often give my clients the answers they seek earlier than expected. If that happens, I refund the unused retainer."

"I take it I didn't set off your warning bells?"

"No, and dial it back, bub. I have a werewolf boyfriend. Plus, I tend to make love slaves out of mortals."

"How do you know I'm not a vampire, too? Or a werewolf?"

"I know."

"How?"

"You have an aura, and I can hear your heart beating in your chest, and I can read your mind."

"You can read minds?"

"Only the minds of mortals."

"I see. What am I thinking now?"

"You are thinking about your social security number."

"Which is?"

"343-726-2978."

"Okay, wow. No, wait. You said you research clients before you meet them. You likely already know my social security number."

"Likely."

"This is so weird."

"Tell me about it."

"The thing is... you guessed that I was thinking about my social security number, and that's pretty amazing in and of itself."

"In and of."

"Okay, let's see... what am I thinking of now?"

"*The Goonies*. You wish they made a sequel. Okay, now you're feeling afraid. And now you think I'm a witch or something. That's actually a good guess."

"You're a witch and vampire?"

"Kinda. Though I'm primarily an energy vampire, I'm sort of getting back my witch mojo, so to speak. Long story."

"What's happening?"

"Oh, did you think I was kidding when I told

you that I was a vampire?"

"Um... I think you are a mind reader or something."

"Not quite, bub. I'm a walking, talking vampire and witch—well, minor witch. I guess I'm also kind of the angel of death, too. But don't worry, I mostly just kill demons. I say mostly because I've recently killed some dark masters, but that's a whole other story."

"Jesus."

"I'm definitely not him. And in case you're wondering, crucifixes never worked on me, though my now dead ex-husband—who is a lowly evolved dark master now possessing my son in a parallel world—had tried to use them on me. He was scared of me. Still is, I think. Which is kinda strange to say, since I cradled his dead body in my arms a few years ago. But I didn't kill him. A rival vampire did. Anywho. Any more questions?"

"Am I sleeping?"

"I doubt it."

"I think I'm dreaming."

"Want me to pinch you and find out?"

"No, it's okay. Wait—No, really, it's okay. Ouch! Shit. You pinched me."

"I did."

"That really hurt."

"I pinch with the best of them. Still think

you're dreaming?"

"No, unless I dreamed you pinched me."

"You can't dream pain."

"Who says?"

"Evolution. The body and mind are designed to awaken when feeling—or dreaming—of pain. It's why you can't burn to death in your sleep."

"I'm not sure I've ever heard of that."

"Look it up."

"Um, maybe later. How did we go down this road?"

"You asked about my business set up. You questioned it. You also seemed to suggest that I was foolish to allow complete strangers into my home, strangers who have real world problems. You had a tone. I decided to set you straight."

"By telling me you're a vampire with a warning system in place?"

"Yes. Did that help clear things up?"

"Um, maybe I should go."

"Maybe. But when will you ever talk to another living—well kind of living—vampire again?"

"I'm not sure what to say to that."

"I'm saying, you are sitting across from an immortal, a woman who has spoken to the Origin of all life in the Universe, killed the devil himself, is friends with witches and werewolves and fairies, whose son just might be an angel in training, and whose daughter is telepathic enough to read minds around the world, and you just want to leave?"

"Yes, very much so."

"Are you sure you want to go?"

"Yes, no. Now I don't know."

"Did you see what I did there? I gave you a small suggestion to stay. Can't you tell the new desire didn't really come from you?"

"Um, I dunno. I did want to go, very badly. But now, the idea of staying here with you sounds not so terrible."

"Gee thanks."

"You… you compelled me to think this way?"

"I did."

"And you can compel me to…"

"Do anything I want, yes."

"Even kill myself?"

"Wow, that went dark fast. But I suppose I could if I really laid it on thick. But I'm not that kind of person. Not all vampires are psychotic."

"That's good to know. How… how many of you are there?"

"Like me? Millions—oh, you don't mean in that multiverse kind of way."

"No, but maybe we can get back to the multiverse…?"

"I'd rather not. It makes my head spin. And to answer your question… I really don't know how many of us there are. A few thousand, likely."

"And werewolves? You said your boyfriend was one?"

"He is, and there might be less of those suckers. Otherwise, you'd hear more stories of bodies being torn to shreds on nights of the full moon. Or even more people straight up disappearing. Luckily, most wolf men tend to lock themselves down on such nights. I know my honey does."

"Does what, exactly?"

"Seals himself in a cell below his house, with the help of his butler who might just be the inspiration for the real Frankenstein monster."

"Jesus."

"I thought we covered him."

"What did I walk into here?"

"A vampire's den, so to speak. Or, more accurately, a vampire's home office. An office you questioned, mind you. So, in effect, your questions led us here."

"But..."

"But you weren't expecting all this?"

"Would anyone?"

"Maybe a few in my circle of friends. Yours, not so much."

"You really a vampire?"

"An energy vampire now; a blood vampire for over a decade."

"Why the change?"

"It's a long story."

"I wouldn't mind hearing—yes, a long story. I will let it go. Say, did you just compel me to let it go?"

"I did."

"Wow. And now I have no interest in the story. Like, I barely even remember which story I'm talking about. How did you do that?"

"Intent and focus and magic. Also, some technical know-how. I had to learn to do this. And once I learned how to do it, I had to get over the ethical issue of using it."

"I take it the moral issues have gone out the window?"

"Yes and no. I don't take pleasure in forcing someone to do something against their will—and be glad that I don't."

"Otherwise I could be dancing in front of you like a fool?"

"Except you wouldn't think you were a fool. You would think you were doing something to make me happy, and you would dance until I told you to stop."

"Or until I dropped dead with exhaustion?"

"Yes. But, as discussed, I'm not that kind of

vampire."

"You don't seem to have much problem changing my mind."

"It's a sliding scale. If I don't think my suggestion is traumatic or intrusive, then I'm fine with it. But it took me awhile to get to this place. Usurping someone's will is no small thing."

"But you do it anyway?"

"When I see fit."

"And this no longer bothers you?"

"Not like it used to."

"Would it bother you to make me hurt myself?"

"Yes, unless I had good reason to. If that was the case, then no."

"Are other vampires looser with their morals?"

"No doubt. But vampires don't like to draw attention to themselves."

"Why's that?"

"There are hunters out there."

"Vampire hunters?"

"Yes. And should they detect that a vampire is behaving badly, they will come for him or her."

"And kill them?"

"Yes."

"So, there is a check and balance to the

system?"

"Yes."

"That gives me some relief."

"It should."

"Are you growing tired of my questions?"

"Not yet. I sense your concern and curiosity. I'm glad you stayed."

"Did I have a choice?"

"Yes and no. If you truly wanted to leave, I would have allowed it. But you weren't as afraid as you thought you were. Just freaked out a little."

"Are you controlling me right now?"

"No."

"Good, because it's nice knowing the world is a little more interesting than I realized twenty minutes ago. Weird as it sounds, I like knowing that there are vampires in the world. And werewolves. And demons... and what else did you say?"

"Angels and fairies. There are gods and goddesses and lake monsters, and so much more."

"You said you killed the devil?"

"I did."

"I find that hard to believe."

"Then let me show you—"

"Show me?"

"Yes. Now be quiet."

***

"Okay, wow. That... was disturbing. Was that really the devil?"

"Yup."

"He looked terrible... and massive."

"The devil doesn't fight fair."

"I can see that. You were flying. You had wings. And you disappeared and reappeared."

"Sometimes I don't fight fair, either."

"Were those hooded things... demons?"

"Yes."

"And those lighted beings?"

"Angels."

"And the giant black wolf?"

"A werewolf in his wolf form."

"Your boyfriend, I presume?"

"Yup. My beautiful hairball."

"Those lightning bolts I saw?"

"My witchy friend at work."

"Okay, last but not least... what was that giant, fiery creature with the fire sword?"

"Oh, that's just my son."

"Is he always, um, burning?"

"Only when he's protecting his mama. I suspect he might be an angel in training. And get this, my witch friend thinks he might actually be an archangel in training."

"I don't know what to say."

"I don't either."

"I just came here to see if you could help me find out if my wife is cheating on me."

"I know. And we will. But you asked the right question. A snobby question, mind you."

"Sorry. It's just that a home office didn't make a lot of sense to me, especially with what appeared to be bedrooms down the hallway. But now I get it. There likely isn't much that worries you. Truth is, clients should be afraid of coming here!"

"Most don't get the behind the curtain look that you got."

"Lucky me."

"Maybe, maybe not."

"No, I feel lucky. Unless you're going to eat me or something."

"I don't drink blood. But I could deplete you so thoroughly of energy that you slip forever into a coma."

"Wow, okay. I'm happy you are a good vampire."

"I'm just me, though it took some work to fight off the dark master within. Like most dark masters, she had a corrupting influence."

"Should I ask about these dark masters?"

"Probably not, but I will say this... they are the source of much pain."

"What are they?"

"Dark magicians. So dark they have found a way to defy the cycle of life and death. Hence, immortality."

"Did you say one such entity is in your son?"

"Yes. His father's soul."

"Should I ask?"

"No."

"Fine. So these dark masters... what's their story? Maybe you can give me the shortened version?"

"Sure, why not? Let's see, there are a number of factions of them. The biggest is led by an entity who once possessed me. Her name is Elizabeth."

"And is she why you were forced to drink blood?"

"Yes."

"And with her gone, you are now an energy vampire?"

"Yes, very good. Also, with her gone, I can once again practice magic. I'm a budding witch now, but I'm not very good at it. Like, it's not coming easy to me."

"I'm sorry to hear that."

"It is what it is. Trust me, I'm not complaining. I've got other gifts."

"The wings and disappearing thing?"

"And teleporting, and mind reading, and enhanced strength, speed, hearing and sight. Oh, and I occasionally turn into a rather large, blunt-nosed dragon, which is summoned from the fourth dimension."

"Your life sounds boring. I'm sorry."

"Okay, that made me laugh. Brownie point for you."

"Are you going to kill me, now that you've told me all this?"

"No."

"Are you going to make me forget all this?"

"Oh, yeah."

"Any way I can convince you not to?"

"Nope."

"Fine. So, for a brief period in my life, I am being given a glimpse into this world. Better than nothing, I'll take it."

"Good outlook."

"What was meeting god like?"

"Not really god. It calls itself the Origin, and it's the source of all life in the universe and beyond."

"And you met him... or it? Face to face?"

"I did. And it was life-changing, to say the least—surreal, beautiful and heartbreaking."

"Why heartbreaking?"

"It was the last I saw of my one-time father from a past life—the vampire sire who ultimately turned me in this life."

"Do you hate him for that?"

"Quite the opposite. I love him with all that I have. A remarkable man. The earth didn't deserve him."

"Is he in heaven?"

"Not exactly. He returned to the Origin, which is to say, he returned to the light. It is my fate as well, should I ever perish."

"You sound sad."

"It's a heavy subject for me."

"But you are immortal..."

"Immortals die, too."

"Wait. I know this one. Silver and a stake?"

"Just silver, through the heart. Thus, death."

"But isn't all death forever, human and immortal?"

"Not quite. The soul eventually reincarnates into a new body."

"And you will not reincarnate?"

"Never again."

"Well, then I wish you a long, long, long life here on planet earth."

"Thank you. That's sweet. Now, we should probably talk about your problem."

"My cheating wife?"

"Yes."

"Does that mean our conversation is over?"

"It does."

"Can I ask one more question?"
"You can."
"Is there any chance I can convince you that I won't tell anyone your secret?"
"Not a chance."
"But I want to remember."
"I know you do."
"I... want... um... hi."
"Hi."
"Are you Samantha Moon?"
"I am."
"I'm here for my 3:00 pm appointment."
"You don't say."
"Wow, you work out of your home?"
"I do."
"I've always wanted to work from my home—you're so lucky. But is it safe to work from..."
"To work from where?"
"Um, I lost my train of thought."
"No worries. So, how can I help you?"
"You're the first private investigator I've ever talked to. I'm kind of nervous."
"Don't be nervous."
"Have we ever met?"
"I don't think so."
"Not sure why I asked that. Suddenly, you don't look familiar at all... wait, what was I just saying?"

"You were going to tell me about your cheating wife."

"Yes, yes of course. Sorry, wow. I didn't mean to yawn so loud."

"It's okay, I just needed a little snack."

"Snack?"

"Never mind."

"Yes, never mind. What were we talking about again? Oh, yes, my wife..."

The End

J.R. RAIN

Moon Quiz

Author's Note: Moon Quiz

"Moon Quiz" takes place shortly after the events in *Moon Dance*, the first book in the main series.

~~~~~

"Next question, Sam."

"No, please. No more questions."

"C'mon, just a few more. Pretty please. This is fun."

"For you," I mumble into my glass of wine.

We are at my sister's house, drinking white zinfandel and watching *Big Brother* while the kids play video games upstairs. Rick, Mary Lou's husband, is in his office, grading papers. Danny, of course, is AWOL. So, a typical night.

"Please, Sam."

"Fine. One more."

"Yay. There's just a few left."

"I said one—"

"Okay, let's see..." My sister is reading from

a tattered copy of *Cosmo* that she'd swiped from her dentist's office. I reminded her that that was stealing. She'd shrugged it off and said, 'So, sue me,' which led me to remind her that the police didn't sue; they arrested. She'd only waved me off and poured us more wine.

At the moment, I can't help but notice that my face doesn't reflect in my half-empty wine glass. I hold it up a little higher, looking deeper into it. Nope. Nothing. Maybe a hint of some of the makeup I'm wearing, but that's about it. I stick my tongue out... and still nothing. How the hell is my tongue invisible, too?

I sigh, suddenly depressed.

"If you're done screwing around with your glass, we can continue."

"I need something stronger," I say.

"Stronger how—oh, no. You mean blood?"

"Yup."

"No blood for you!" she says suddenly, slapping her hand on the counter, and imitating the Soup Nazi from *Seinfeld*.

"Oh, brother."

"Next question: Would you like to be famous?"

"Not anymore," I answer.

"Did you used to want to be?"

I think about that. "No, not really. I was happy being a federal ag—"

"No, I mean before that."

"How much before?"

"When you were a kid. Say, in middle school. You know, before you became jaded by life."

"Who said I was jaded?"

"Who just said they needed something stronger?"

"Fine," I say, and think back. Way back. "I wanted to be a singer. And a clown."

My sister giggles. "A singing clown?"

"Sure. Why not?"

"How did I not know this?"

"Because you were in high school, and you had boobs, and you were dating boys. Oh, and you never asked."

"Still, I think I would have known if my kid sister wanted to be a clown."

I shrug. "Next question."

"We're going to circle back to this clown business."

"Fine, whatever."

She scans the magazine, finds her place. "Ooh, here's a good one. Do you have a secret hunch about how you will die?"

I blink. "That question is in *Cosmo*?"

"Sure is."

She flips the magazine around and points with a freshly manicured nail. I give it only a passing scan, since I obviously believe my sister. I wave my hand. "Fine, fine."

"Well? What's your answer?"

I had, of course, noticed that the first few questions had *two* tick marks next to them, and the remaining questions only had one. Meaning, my sister had already taken the questionnaire. My sister needs to get a life.

"Doesn't apply," I say, shrugging. "I'm immortal. I'm going to live forever."

"Ooh, look at me," teases my sister. "I'm immortal. I won't die."

"Well, unless someone stabs me in the heart with a silver dagger," I say.

"Okay, this just got dark."

"Just saying."

"What about a wooden stake?" she asks, eyes narrowing.

I shake my head. "I honestly don't know. I'm new at this, remember? Silver, I know, hurts like hell."

Truth is, my pal Fang believes that the whole wooden stake business is all wrong. According to him, only silver can harm vampires—or other immortals. Still, a wooden stake to the heart would hurt... so... damn... much.

Mary Lou sets her pen down. "You're never going to die."

"Maybe not."

"You really are going to live forever."

"That's what they say. This is news to you?"

"Well, I never... Sam, do you have any idea how long that is?"

"Pretty long."

"Think about it, sweetie. Five hundred years from now... you'll still be alive. And I will be only a memory. All of us will only be a memory. Me, your kids, everyone."

"Unless you join me," I say.

"Oh, posh. I would make a terrible vampire. No thank you. I mean, look at your nails."

I shrug. "Your loss."

She grabs her pen again. "Next question. If a crystal ball could tell you the truth about yourself, your life, the future or anything else, what would you want to know?"

"If my kids will be okay."

My sister nods. "I get that. But what about for you?"

I think about it long and hard, sipping from my wine and listening to our kids upstairs. I can hear Anthony laughing and slapping the floor the way he does when he's happy. Tammy is up there, too, but I can't hear her. Maybe because she's not a hyperactive boy.

I shrug. "Nothing else matters."

"What about between you and Danny?"

"What about me and Danny?"

"Don't you want to know how things will turn out?"

I set my empty glass down. I suspect I know how things will turn out. "No. Next question."

Mary Lou takes some air and clearly doesn't approve. What she doesn't approve of, I don't know. Maybe my outlook on life. But if you're going to live forever, why worry about yourself? And why worry about a cheating husband I'm going to far outlive anyway? Like she said, Danny will someday be a distant memory. Of course, I can say that about my kids, too, which breaks my heart more than I can handle right now.

"Last question," says Mary Lou. "Are you an arm girl or a chest girl?"

The question makes me laugh, thankfully. It also gets me thinking about Kingsley Fulcrum's arms. Those inhumanly big arms. I briefly wonder what they would feel like wrapped around me, holding me close. They would, I think, feel perfect. And hairy.

"I'm definitely an arm girl," I say.

"Really?"

"Really."

"What about butts... chests?"

"Give me a pair of loving arms, and I'm good."

Mary Lou makes a final check in the magazine and tosses it aside. She also makes a face. "Other than sounding like a bad Western song, we're done here." She picks up her glass, raises it, then pauses halfway to her mouth. "A clown, really?"

"Clowns are fun," I say. "Even blood-sucking clowns."

"Thanks for that," says Mary Lou. "Now, I'm going to have nightmares."

Upstairs, the laughing turns to yelling, and the thumping on the floor turns into a full-on wrestling match. Mary Lou sighs. "Am I taking this one, or are you?"

I wink. "I think we both know the answer to that one."

"Bitch," she says, but leans over and hugs me.

Super tight, and with a lot of love.

Yeah, I needed that.

The End

Moon Beast

1.

"Say again?" I ask.

"We think our park is home to a monster," says the council member.

"A monster?"

"Yes."

"You say that with a straight face."

"Trust me, I don't want to, but it appears to be true."

"Okay. What kind of monster?"

"The kind that could leave behind this."

The muscular man behind the table pushes a photograph toward me. His arms, I note, ripple nicely. More than nicely. Sweet mama. He's rolled the sleeves of his dress shirt up well above his elbows, accentuating the ripples. The woman sitting next to him, his colleague on the Norco City Council, leans in close to get a look at the picture. A little too close. I suspect she takes every opportunity she can to lean into those arms.

I'm at the city offices on Main Street, in a

town a hop, skip, and jump from Fullerton. Norco sports lots of rolling, sun-baked hills and enough traffic to make one want to hang oneself. Being one of the first cities out of Orange County, in the slightly more rural Riverside County, Norco offers the promise of cheaper housing if one is willing to pay the price of traffic. Judging by how long it took me to get out here, I'm guessing many were willing to pay the price.

In the photo is a blood-red print with three splayed toes, one of which seems to have curled in on itself. Next to it is a man's foot for scale. The man is wearing yellow, low top Converse All Stars. Obviously, he's as cool as cool gets... whoever he is.

Actually, upon closer inspection, I'm not convinced these are three toes. More like one big roundish print, with blood—or paint—being flung before it.

"Is that blood?" I ask, thanking the good Lord my stomach no longer growls at such imagery. Wanna feel like a ghoul? Try salivating every time something bloody flashes across the TV screen.

"We're not sure. The material disappears before we can test it."

"Is this the only print?"

The man shakes his head. "There is usually

a trail of them."

"How many prints in total?"

"Dozens of them, every morning. But they're usually gone before noon."

"Gone?"

The man—Wade—nods. It looks like it pains him. What pains him, I think, is acknowledging these prints exist in the first place. "They fade away. Right before our eyes. I've seen it myself. They leave no residue, no stain, nothing. Just... gone."

"And you've taken samples?"

Mary, the woman, nods. "All samples disappear, too."

"It's just after nine now," I say. "Will the prints still be there?"

Wade nods. "Likely. They tend to disappear around ten or eleven. It's why we called you in so early, so you can head out there after and take a look at them... before they vanish, of course. The park's maintenance crew blocked the area off from the public."

"Has anyone seen or heard who might have left these prints behind?"

The two council members look at each other for a heartbeat or two before Wade finally shrugs. "Nothing definitive. We're getting, um, dubious reports at this point."

"How do you know they are dubious?"

"Because they're vastly different. We're getting Bigfoot reports, dinosaur reports, Chthulu reports—whatever the hell that is."

"An elder god," I say without thinking. They both stare at me. "Sorry, my son plays a lot of video games. I had this same conversation with him a few months ago. I've been updated on all the old gods."

Wade and his bulging arms seem tense. "Remember, this is a public park. In the middle of our city. We have trees, yes, but not enough to conceal a Bigfoot or dinosaur or...

"Elder god."

"Yes, that."

Mary says, "Well, it sounds like we have the right person. We asked around and one name kept coming up. Samantha Moon, private eye. Apparently, you've helped a number of police departments in the area on a handful of their, um, off the radar weird cases."

"I'm a sort of an off the radar kind of detective."

"Then count us in," says Mr. Sun's Out/Guns Out. "We want to hire you to get to the bottom of this. We need you to find out who or what is leaving behind these prints. We need you to find the so-called Beast of Santana Park. Or so the newspaper is already calling it."

"And if I do find it?"

"Get rid of it, whatever it is."

"Getting rid of it might cost you extra."

His arms ripple with agitation. "Fine. Whatever. Just help us. Please."

"Yes, please," says Mary. "I walk in that park. Now, I don't. Others are staying away, too."

"Well, we can't have that," I say. "I'll see what I can do."

I take a moment to say my goodbyes to Thing #1 and Thing #2... that is, his right and left arms.

Then head out to the park.

2.

"Wow," I say.

"That's what we've been saying for the past few days. Actually, we use stronger words than wow."

"I'm sure you do."

I'm standing with one of the park maintenance guys. He's dressed in khakis and a tan work shirt with the Norco logo above the chest pocket. The name on his shirt says 'Miguel.' Before us are twenty or thirty bloody prints stretching along a slightly curved cement walking path between two adjacent Little League baseball fields. Interestingly, there seems to be only a left print, as though something monstrous has been hopping on one leg. Then again, this could be an indication of a hoax. Like some teens only had one fake left foot. Of course, it doesn't explain why the red liquid would fade hours later. Also, the prints seem to materialize on the path and head east. Yellow caution tape surrounds them, giving them a big berth, keeping the looky-loos away.

And I think I'm right about my earlier assessment. These aren't so much three-toed prints as something being splattered, dragged or flung forward. Or something bleeding badly.

I check the time... just after 9:30 a.m. "When did the prints first appear this morning?"

Miguel shrugs. "They were here when I got here."

"What time was that?"

"Seven."

"Any idea when the prints were made?"

"Some time during the night, be my guess."

"I take it you didn't see a Bigfoot wandering around when you got here."

He smiles. "No."

I leave Miguel behind and follow the prints. They do have a slightly Jurassic feel to them, like something monstrous made them, rather than kids perpetuating a prank. Then again, they have a demonic feel too. If these aren't a prank, then something big made them, especially considering the length of the stride... easily three times the length of my own. Does that make the creature nearly twenty feet tall? Maybe.

I drop to a knee next to one print to get a closer look at it. With eyes watching me beyond the yellow tape, and all too aware some cell phone cameras were rolling, I reach down and dip my right index finger into the pool of red. My fingertip comes away gleaming crimson and feeling cold. I sniff it and get nothing. Maybe Kingsley could have gotten something from the ichor's scent. If anything, the lack of smell is telling, too. I rub the goo between my thumb and forefinger. Sticky, like semi-dry glue.

I continue following the prints until they veer off into the grass. The sun is bright, the day clear. In the far corner of the wraparound parking lot, I spot what looks like an aerobic class. Again... in the parking lot. Nearby, a group of four guys play a sort of reverse volleyball game, slamming something into the grass and trying to hit it on the rebound. Not sure what game it is, but it looks fun. The park itself is on the slope of a gradually rising foothill, ultimately leading to the bigger mountains surrounding Norco. This is the affluent part of Norco, which is probably why I was called in to nip this 'monster footprint thing' in the bud. Then again, something like this could bring in tourists by the boatload. Just ask Loch Ness.

And yeah, there is a chance I might have uncovered the secret behind Loch Ness.

But, shh. I'm not telling. I doubt the city wants their upscale park known for a monster, especially one that leaves behind bloody footprints.

Of course, this could always just be a prank, perhaps even a magical prank. There could be some young witches and warlocks nearby cooking up trouble in their cauldrons. Although my witchy abilities are gradually returning to me, I am still not proficient enough with them to get a sense of if there is magic involved here.

I might need to call in the big guns. And by big guns, I mean Allison—not Wade's arms. She has a sixth sense for this kind of stuff. The problem is, she lives in Beverly Hills, and I am out in Norco, nearly an hour and a half away.

Then again, distance is nothing a little teleportation couldn't resolve. I am not done here yet. I mentally summon Miguel to come meet me in the grass. As he ambles over, I note the red stuff is still on my fingers. Miguel seems a tad confused as to why he came over. I remove the confusion and ask if the park has cameras.

"Just some cameras in the parking lot."

"Has anyone reviewed the footage?"

"The police. They found nothing. But, as you can see, there is no gate around the park. Anyone could access the park from the sidewalks."

"Has any evidence been found that would suggest this is a prank? Paint cans? Paint brushes? Something left behind?" Of course, the liquid is far more translucent than paint. Truth is, I've never actually seen a substance like this. Since there is no evidence of a mortally wounded animal lying around here, I had to assume this to be a prank.

"Nothing that I know of."

"Has anyone seen anything suspicious?"

"I am but a humble maintenance man. No one tells me anything."

"And the prints always fade away?"

"For the last two days. And if you look, they're fading now. Always happens around this time."

Son on a bitch, he is right of course. The prints are sort of shrinking inward, but slowly. I look at my thumb and forefingers. Yup, the gooiness there is thinning out, too.

I continue following the prints through the

grass, to where they disappear in the middle of the field. I note the grass does not appear affected by whoever left the print behind—no flattening, for instance. Just the blood-like substance.

I turn in a circle, scanning. Yup, the tracks end here. They start on the cement path, and wind up in the field, just beyond the home run fence. Probably a distance of about fifty yards total.

What the hell is going on?

As I stand there, hands on hips, the sun high overhead, and people watching me from beyond the yellow tape, the red prints in the grass slowly, slowly disappear. Ten minutes later, they are gone completely.

As if they were never there.

3.

I next meet with a Norco beat cop at a donut shop called Baker's Dozen.

I ask if he is trying to be a living cliché. He shrugs and explains that they give him free donuts... what is he supposed to do? Go somewhere and pay, like a normal human being? I tell him he has a point and we get down to business. According to Officer Jenkins, no other bloody prints have been found in the city. No one has been hurt in or around the park in the past week, either, when the prints first started appearing. He has no credible witnesses, and no evidence. I ask if he has any theories, and he has none.

I tell him he has sprinkle in his cop mustache and he thanks me, and I leave the city of Norco.

After all, I have a friend to meet.

4.

We are at a place called Fuddruckers in Buena Park, where the burgers are good, the condiments copious, and the location about halfway between my house and Fang's apartment in Los Angeles.

"You look good, Moon Dance."

"As do you, Fang."

Maybe it's weird we still use our old AOL aliases—names we used when we both met anonymously a dozen or so years ago in a vampire chat room. Of course, Fang hadn't started out as a vampire when we first met online. Well, not a real vampire. Thanks to a rather strange childhood beset with extremely long canine teeth that caused him undue psychological harm, he had developed an unhealthy obsession with bloodsuckers, even believing he was one. His obsession led to various murders and eventually a prison escape.

Technically, he is still wanted by the police. Technically, my friend Fang might be a borderline psychopath. Luckily, his psychosis has led to a lifetime of researching all things supernatural, knowledge which has proven invaluable for me. Believe it or not, there are some things that can't be found on Google.

Like Kingsley, Fang's inner dark master has elected to stay connected with its host. At least for now. With the destruction of the Void, dark masters are once again free to wander the earth. Of course, to do so, they had to break free of the physical flesh that contained them. Breaking free meant killing their host... or waiting for their host to be killed.

And why would a dark master elect to stay in a host? A myriad of reasons, really. Some hosts and masters are true besties. To be besties takes trust, because once a dark master is allowed freedom, all control is lost. A dark master can, theoretically, take over a body.

In the case with Fang, host and master found a sort of balance... each being given access to the body. This is how Fang exists. As does Dracula.

"How's the business?" I ask him.

"Holding steady. Lost some patrons when the Snap happened."

The Snap being, of course, when the Void collapsed... resulting in some dark masters killing their hosts and breaking free to live life on earth as a sort of spirit on steroids. Meaning, they can manifest anywhere, at any time, often for lengthy periods. Granted, their bodies are ectoplasmic in nature, but certainly do the trick when necessary.

"The good news is, those vampires who chose to stick around tend to be better customers."

"Oh? Why's that?"

"Think about it, Moon Dance. Only the real pieces of shit killed their hosts and split."

"The psychopaths flew the coop."

"Exactly."

"Makes sense. You were left with better people all around. More balanced."

"Speaking of which, where is Elizabeth now?"

"My guess... planning on taking over some unused space in the universe."

"Like a god."

"Exactly as a god. Remember, half of the

Origin is still unknown."

"Thus, the unused space."

"Yes."

"And she hopes to fill it how?"

"With a universe of her own."

"But she was once a human being. How can she be a god?"

"With the help of a creator. Or perhaps many creators."

"That's a scary thought."

"Maybe the scariest."

We get on to the topic of the footprints, of which I show him a picture.

"I'm fairly certain it's made of blood... except it keeps disappearing. Or if not blood, it could be a form of disappearing ink. Or even be a form of magic or alchemy."

"So no scientific tests have been done?"

"Not yet. Any samples would have disappeared."

"No residue left behind?"

"None that I could see. Likely, the city's next step is to test at the park. I think they're hoping I can give them some answers before science is called in. I take it you haven't heard of such a creature?"

"Sorry, Moon Dance. But I have heard of hauntings leaving behind blood... and for it to disappear later. The blood, that is."

He tells me more. A friend of his in Naples, Florida had such an experience in, of all places, her water heater closet in her condo. For a crazy week or two, every time she reached into the closet for a broom or mop, her hand came out covered in blood. From her forearm to her fingertips. *Dripping*, too. All over her floor. It covered the towels she used to clean the stuff off. And then, a few hours later, it disappeared. His friend had taken copious pictures, many of which Fang had seen.

"Is this a mortal friend?"

"Yes, and I see where you're going with this. A mortal might have... tasted said blood?"

"Not like it would hurt us, and would be a good test."

"The taste test." Fang nods. "Sure, I would have. Why not? Unless the blood was infused with silver. But even then, it would only make us sick. But no, she was a mortal. A friend from the asylum."

I nod, knowing well his story of having killed his girlfriend by drinking her blood... all while he had been very mortal. A true glimpse into his madness. All because of two extraordinary long—and natural—canine teeth. Teeth that had been the bane of his existence early in life, until he embraced them.

"You stayed in touch with a fellow inmate?"

"Not an inmate."

I blink. "A guard?"

"Yes."

"From the prison you escaped from?"

Fang shrugs his narrow shoulders. "What can I say? She took pity on me when they forcibly removed my teeth. To say I was devastated would be an understatement. I was catatonic. She spoke to me often. Or tried to. Said I reminded her of her son. Said she was sorry they had done that to me. I took advantage of her kindness, manipulated it, got her to agree to help me in ways that are not important now. But just know doors were unlocked, cameras were turned off, and guards were diverted. She didn't want to help me. I worked on her until she finally agreed. I had to kill one of her fellow workers. We both knew that had to happen."

"Boy, you were quite the charmer even without the power of influence."

"I did what I had to do to escape. Remarkably, she had covered her tracks well and ultimately returned to her home state of Florida. I would look her up many years later, and we would have many secret meetings. Friendly meetings. In fact, she would help me become the man I am today. Turned out, security guards in prison know a lot of criminally minded individuals. With her help, I truly started a new life."

That she helped a young guy completely off his rocker with murder in his heart, didn't say much about her moral code. But not everyone on planet Earth is a saint.

"Are you thinking these prints are paranormal then? Perhaps even ectoplasmic in nature?" I ask.

"Would explain why they disappear. Oh, and to finish off my friend's story... turned out she had the mother of all hauntings. An angry ghost. Took a ton of sage, prayers, priests, and a vampire who could see into the spirit world."

"Would that vampire be you?"

"Yeah, turned out an entire family had been killed there. Three kids, the mom and the dad."

"Holy hell."

"Exactly. The father had been straight up possessed by a demon. Happened after your battle with the devil, when his demons split the coop, so to speak."

"I'm hunting them down all the time. Turns out the devil created a crap-ton of demons."

"And some of the bastards found refuge in humans. Weak humans, those susceptible to possession, and I'm not talking dark masters here. I'm talking demonic possession, which is a completely different kind of possession. Meaning, demons can be ejected, though they can also cause a lot of problems."

"Back to the prints, could this creature be a ghost?"

"Maybe. Then again, it could be a young witch or wizard playing a clever trick. But my money is on something dead... and something massive. And likely very, very old."

5.

I'm home again.

And by home, I mean my simple four-bedroom house in Fullerton with its frustratingly detached garage and chain link fence around the front yard, and the glowing Pep Boys sign overlooking the backyard. The house is in a cul-de-sac, which means the property lines in my front and back yards aren't at even angles. The property is sort of wedge-shaped, which results in us having a rather massive backyard, complete with three orange trees.

As I hang my keys on the hook by the front door, shrug out of my light jacket and toss it over the back of one of the chairs around the small kitchen table, I wonder again why I didn't keep the massive home bequeathed to me by my vampire sire and one-time father.

The problem being, it was also a little creepy. Which is saying a lot, coming from a vampire. The old couple living in it as caretakers are as strange as strange gets. Plus, the place is filled to the brim with spirits. Any mortal would have run out screaming, never to return. Part of me thinks Fang bought it to do me a favor. Then again, the home is situated in the Fullerton Hills, with a panoramic view of the city and certainly befitting a vampire.

The home is Fang's second now. His getaway of sorts. He lives in an apartment in the city, close to his business. Methinks he has designs on setting up a similar blood hub in Orange County. That, and he likely wanted to be closer to me. Guys like Fang don't care much about me having a boyfriend. His obsession runs deep. And Fang can obsess with the best of them. Then again, whether he is obsessed with me or not doesn't really matter. I like Fang. I can handle Fang. Plus, he is kind of cute in a psychopathic kind of dead-stare way.

Since returning home from our whirlwind tour of Europe, Tammy and her elven boyfriend have been inseparable. I reminded Kai that my daughter was only 17 and he was like 200 years old. Though he was considered a young adult in his culture, my implication was obvious. Hands off until she was at least an adult—and better if it was a good deal longer than that. My daughter had, of course, turned beet red during this entire exchange, pleading with me to shut the hell up. I ignored her completely.

Kai assured me he would never do anything to upset me. I looked at Tammy when he said that, and she could not have appeared more thrilled. My daughter was two months shy of her eighteenth birthday, and she had already found her true love? Well, who was I to get in the way of destiny?

I can hear Anthony in his bedroom, playing a video game by the sounds of it. As I stand there in the foyer, the house quiet save for my son, I suddenly have an overwhelming urge to talk to his father. Like we used to do back in the day when we discussed life, our kids, everything. Kingsley is a good one to talk to about, well, everything. But I hadn't created my kids with Kingsley. He doesn't have a vested interest in them, not like Danny.

I move through the living room, turn left at the hallway and knock on my son's door. With no response, I knock louder. With still no response, I close my eyes as tight as I can and open the door.

"Ant?"

"Oh, hey ma! Geez, why do you always come into my room with your eyes closed?"

MOON SHOTS

I peek an eye open. He sits on the floor—his favorite seat in the house—with his headset askew, one ear exposed. He keeps playing his game, light flashing over his face, even as he looks from me to the screen.

His question is so innocent and sweet, that I don't want to cloud his pure thoughts for the real reason I come in eyes wide shut. "Oh, you know. You might be changing or something."

"Oh, okay, ma. Nope, just playing Angel Gate and talking to Dad."

"Yes, about that... would you mind terribly if I spoke to... your dad?"

"You want to talk to pops?"

"You call him pops now?"

"He likes it. Says it reminds him of his own dad."

"Um, okay."

"He says he would like to talk to you, too, that it's been too long. Just give me a sec. I need to save the game and sort of quiet my mind."

Sadly, I know why he has to quiet his mind. It is so that Danny can take over his body, completely and totally. I don't like it. Hate it, in fact. But then again, I requested the meeting, and it is the only way to talk to Danny without my son being a go-between. It also means, in theory, Danny can keep on taking over his son's body, by not giving it up. Such is the fate of the vamps who allow their dark master even the slightest bit of freedom.

And so, feeling sick to my stomach, I watch as my little fire warrior takes off the headset, nods as if he is having an internal conversation —which he likely is—and scoots until his back is pressed against his wooden bed frame and its clever use of drawers. Our house is a small four-bedroom house. We make good use of extra space here.

He looks at me once, smiles in a heart-breaking way, and closes his eyes. I know Danny and Anthony have a good relationship. My daughter attests to that, reporting to me that Danny and Anthony have only normal conversation. His father encourages him in all good things, guiding him with a light hand, and showing kindness and as much wisdom as he can when Anthony asks for help.

So, yeah. Mixed emotions.

Anthony's head bobs forward a number of times, then jerks back suddenly, then falls forward again, chin now resting on his chest. A moment passes, then another. Anthony's chest expands... then keeps on expanding. Someone is taking one helluva deep breath. After another minute of this, Anthony raises his head up and turns toward me. He smiles—but not in that creepy demon-possessed way I have seen. No, despite his failings, Danny isn't a demon. This is a slightly crooked smile, combined with an arrogant lift of one corner of the lip. Arrogant and maybe even ironic. I could never figure that out about Danny. But here it is again, after all these years.

"Hi, Sam," he says.

"Hi, Danny."

"You look well."

"And you look like our son."

"Touché."

He stares down at Anthony's hands, opening and closing them slowly. The difference in my son's eyes is minute but noticeable. My son doesn't squint, but Danny did... and is doing so now. My kid is wide-eyed and innocent, excited to be alive. The person behind these eyes feels entitled. Maybe even arrogant, though Danny never had any reason to be arrogant. Sure, he was an attorney, but not a very successful one. He was a personal injury lawyer, which is to say a glorified claims adjuster.

"You wanted to speak to me, Sam?"

I nod. "First, where's Anthony?"

"He's right here, not very far away."

"Is he scared?"

"Hold on." Danny blinks, blinks again, then opens his eyes wide. "I'm right here, mom.

Don't worry! Me and pops are good!"

"Okay, sweetie. I want to talk to your dad about something important, but private. Will you lock yourself in a sound-proof room?"

"Sure, I can do that. But how will I know when to come out? Never mind. Dad says he'll come get me."

"Thank you, sweetie."

Seconds later, Danny is here again. "So, what can I do for you, Sammie?"

I study him for a moment, collecting my thoughts. "How are you?"

"I'm trapped inside our son's body, but other than that I'm fine."

"Hell isn't real, you know. You needn't have feared it."

"I didn't know that at the time. Plus... I wasn't ready to leave the kids yet."

But he *had* been ready to leave me; after all, he had helped plan my ambush under the Los Angeles River. An ambush that had gotten him killed.

"When do you think you will be ready to leave?" I ask.

"Is that why you called me up, Sam? Is that why you sequestered your son?"

I nod. "Yes. Danny, I've been getting a... feeling that your time with Anthony might be coming to an end."

"Where's this feeling coming from?"

"Hard to know. I'm not generally one to be psychic."

"Very well. To answer your question... I don't know. But weirdly, I've been getting the same feeling. It's why I spend so much time talking to him."

"Do you ever talk to Tammy?"

"I do, when she wants to talk. Lately, she's gone radio silent, as they say."

I nod. "She's been spending a lot of time with that boy."

"The boy who's not a boy."

"What do you think of him?" I ask.

"I don't like him."

"Him personally, or because he's seeing our daughter?"

"Because he's not human. Is that... species-ist of me?"

I shrug. "Yeah, maybe. He's a nice boy."

"But that's just the thing, he's not a boy. He's 200 years old."

"Which is a young adult in their world."

"But what does that mean in our world?"

"I don't know, but Tammy says his intentions are pure and noble."

"Makes me want to scream, Sammie."

"Except you have no mouth to scream."

"I do now."

"Well?"

"Fine, I won't scream. But this is highly... unusual."

"So is possessing your son's body."

"It's not a possession. It's a... residing place."

"Fine. Well, Tammy is crazy about that boy, and she better than anyone knows someone's true character. I think she loves him, Danny."

"Shit."

"Then again, it's young love. Who knows if it will last? She's also almost an adult. I think we need to let her make her own decision about this."

"Even if she doesn't have a clue what she's doing?"

"She has some clue. Besides, you've met him. He looks and acts like a teen."

"When will we meet his family? Or clan? Or colony? Or whatever the hell they're called."

"You mean, when will I? You're dead, remember."

"Dead-ish. And I'm still a part of this family."

"Do you know how crazy that sounds, Danny? How crazy *we* sound?"

"Crazy or not, it is what it is."

Okay, he has a point about that.

We are silent for a few minutes, when he

says, "I think I will be leaving Anthony, too. I don't know why I know."

"I have the same feeling."

"But the strangest thing is... I sense I will be leaving him, but not leaving him, too."

I shrug. "I just sense the leaving part."

"Any idea when?"

"Soon-ish."

"And you have no idea how or why?" he asks.

I shake my head.

"He's not going to be happy to hear this."

"No," I say. "I don't suppose he will be."

"Sam, there's something I need to tell you... our son isn't... normal."

"Ya think?"

"No. I mean, it's something else. He's attracted the attention of the angels."

"Yes, Ishmael has mentioned he looks out for him."

"No, Sam. Not just your one-time guardian angel. A whole host of angels watch over him now."

"Protecting him?"

"I don't know. I don't think so. Mostly, they speak to him when he sleeps."

"Do you know what they say?"

"Sadly, no"

"Does he remember upon waking?"

"Generally, no. But the few memories he has is of them... training him."

"Training him how?"

"My best guess is to be like them."

"An angel?"

"Perhaps even something more. I get a sense that this is big. But I also get a sense that, uh, something is holding him back, and so they are waiting."

"What's holding him back? Do you know?"

Danny takes in some air. "I do. It's me."

6.

It's late.

At the moment, I'm perusing the incident history of crimes at Santana Park in Norco. There are surprisingly few for such a large park. Then again, it is a fairly new development in the city, nestled in the foothills of the Santa Ana Mountains. Still, a big park to attract any number of riffraff over the years... except that doesn't seem to be the case. Crime is low here, with only a few incidents of muggings. One homeless woman had been found dead here about a decade ago.

On a hunch, I type in "witchcraft" and "rituals" and include the park name. Nothing, other than some Halloween stuff going on for the kids.

Well, crap.

On another hunch, this one a bit stronger, I type in "bloody footprints" and get a few dozen hits regarding the current phenomenon. The town council is right; word is spreading about these prints. Likely, this is going to soon draw major news within days.

I click over to the second and third page. Some Facebook profiles mention the prints here and there. Some teens say they're going to camp overnight and find out who or what is leaving the prints.

I click to the fourth page. The connection to my search terms is weakening, random hits showing up. Fifth page... and lo!

A local newspaper from twenty years ago mentions the bloody prints. They even mention the prints disappearing after a few hours. The police think they're a practical joke. Per the article, the prints appeared for four days straight, then they stopped and haven't returned. I note this is a weekly newspaper, so likely they got the full scoop before publishing the article.

I sit back, a bit stunned. Tonight would be the fourth night.

Would the prints disappear for another

twenty years?

I don't know, but I am not going to wait and see.

Time to catch this thing once and for all.

7.

It's past midnight, and the park is mostly empty.

I say mostly because there are three cars parked in the far corner of the lot. Also, I see flashlights sweeping along one of the cement paths. From up here, with my black wings and me dressed in black, no way in hell someone is spotting me. I am up two hundred feet or more, my wings gently sweeping up and down, keeping me hovering more or less in place.

The flashlights belong to security guards. I can see their uniforms pretty clearly from here. And that car working its way along Ontario Ave is a police cruiser. He turns right onto Kellogg Ave and continues his slow circumvention around the park. At the moment, there are no other people in the park. Likely, the police have long since run off any looky-loos.

Scratch that. I spot some kids creeping along Santana Ave, and now they've turned into the park. No flashlights, dark clothing. The park's lights are at a minimum, and so they duck in under the cover of darkness... well, darkness for mortal eyes. There's three of them, and each, undoubtedly, excited to be out tonight on a monster hunt.

I decide to leave them be. Wouldn't be too hard for me to land behind them and compel them to go home. But why should I deprive them of a night of fun, something they might remember forever. Besides, they have me here to protect them. If things get hairy, I'll send them on, or teleport them to safety. For now, they aren't hurting anyone.

I slowly sweep over the park, though I mostly focus my attention on the spot where the prints had appeared. The security guards, I note, actively avoid that spot.

Hours pass, though my angel wings never tire or falter. I slip into a sort of meditative state. It is just so damn peaceful up here, the cool wind, the stars shining above, my mind at peace. The teens have long since taken to sitting under a tree and talking quietly among themselves.

Perhaps another hour later, something bright begins coalescing on the footpath between the two Little League fields. Something big.

Something very, very big.

8.

And glowing.

If I had to guess, I would say a ghost is materializing in the park below. Maybe the biggest ghost ever.

Like all such specters, it's composed of the light particles that flow continuously through the air—and through everything. The source of which, I always believe, is the Origin itself. Spirits use these particles to manifest, though usually not within a spectrum of light humans can see. Luckily, it is exactly the spectrum of light I see within.

Generally, I've come to ignore such manifestations. For instance, sitting in an old restaurant in downtown Fullerton, I once counted forty-eight such manifestations—in one evening. Most formed and disappeared within seconds. Others sat quietly with the diners, then disappeared again. Sharper, clearer manifestations are generally indicative of a recent death. Hazy, scattered ghosts are generally older in nature. At least, that's been my experience.

Once, while driving through Chino Hills, I saw a ghost *goat* in front of a barn. Yes, a goat.

That was random and cute.

But, I've never seen a ghost *dinosaur* before.

Until now.

9.

Composed of staticy light, it creeps through the park, keeping to the same footpath, its massive tail swishing from side to side. It holds its head high, almost proudly, supported on a long, curved neck dozens of feet long.

I don't have a clue what kind of dinosaur it is, but the word 'brontosaurus' comes to mind —I mean, this sucker is huge.

And for something clearly ancient, it holds its shape surprisingly well. The light around it is splotchy in places, indistinct in others—yet the general shape is there. And that shape is an honest-to-god dinosaur.

I drop down for a closer look and note the blood-smeared prints on the sidewalk. I also note the probable cause for them. A dozen or so wounds appear to cover its massive hind leg, wounds that gush ectoplasmic blood. The wounds don't appear isolated to the rear leg. More appear along its flank, neck, front legs...

and even its tail.

If I had to guess, I would say the big fellow here fell victim to a pack of smaller hunters, perhaps something akin to dino version of hyenas.

Its movements begin to slow, as if it is being dragged down.

My heart breaks for it, as I watch it move through the park, its steps faltering. Its occasionally veers off the path. That it's following in the same general direction as the sidewalk is just a fluke. Had there been no cement path, this giant would still be taking this same route, as it had done long before Santana Park was ever a park.

As it has done since damn near forever.

I hover over it, knowing only I can see this special collection of light particles, knowing that a human would simply shiver should they ever cross paths with this creature.

I fly along its massive left side. I could have just as easily been flying alongside a semi-truck. More wounds form, more chunks of meat being torn free as the old boy had been attacked from all sides. It stumbles next to me, reenacting its death scene, over and over again. For some reason, the big fellow never accepted its death, or didn't know it had died.

Its light body ripples and undulates with

each step. That the creature has maintained its general shape for so long is remarkable. At one hundred years, most human ghosts are but a memory of their former selves. At two hundred, they are usually just mere blobs. I hadn't seen human ghosts go back more than a few hundred years, really. Although I do see random, amorphous blobs that appear and disappear. For all I know, those could be our Neanderthal ancestors.

But this fellow has to be 100 million years old or older... yet it has retained its shape, even down to the muscles rippling along its shoulders.

At present, it is about halfway to the point where the prints usually disappear in the grass. History suggests that this would be the last night of its appearance. Would it again disappear for another twenty years, only to return and make this lonely, pitiful walk for four nights? Has it lost all grasp of time? In its mind, is it making the walk every day... except its "days" have now stretched to decades?

Likely, this may not be an actual sentient ghost, but an emotional imprint of a death burned into the environment that replays the same exact events over and over again.

But... it had done so for long, and in such clarity... that perhaps there is something more here. An inkling of intelligence.

Its head drops lower, swinging from side to side. It limps and bleeds. As it has done seemingly forever. I decide to make an executive decision here. It is time to help the big guy go to the light, to return to the Origin. It is time for him to stop bleeding and hurting and dying.

And to go home. Wherever that might be.

10.

I fly under its long, swooping neck and land on the path before it, tucking my wings in.

The beast—likely a brontosaurus—doesn't appear to see me, and why would it? Likely, it has made this walk thousands, if not hundreds of thousands of times, and no doubt rarely saw much more than a squirrel or field mouse appear. Maybe even a park goer... you know, millions of years later. To think that this creature has literally witnessed the rise and fall of the dinos, the eruption of mammals, and finally the hairless, two-footed primates, is surreal at best. I mean, this thing has watched the earth evolve.

Then again, modern humans have only populated this plot of land for maybe a few thousand years. Likely, this giant ghost lizard has not seen too many humans, if ever. And if it often appeared in the middle of the night, the chances of seeing humans decreased significantly.

All of which suggests that this thing would have no clue as to what I was. That is, if it could even see me. Perhaps even sadder, it also means that it hasn't been seen or acknowledged in a hundred million years.

The thing has been alone for damn near the entire course of existence on earth.

It continues forward, forcing me aside. If it sees me, it doesn't show it. Likely, it isn't looking where it's going, so ingrained is this path in its memory.

I dash in front of it again and jump up, shouting and waving my arms.

Nothing. No response, no acknowledgment, no slowing down of its inevitable destination across the field of grass, where likely it will die of its wounds, again and again.

Forevermore.

I consider summoning Talos, who is about the same size as this thing, maybe a little smaller. But I don't want to terrify the old fellow, either. The sudden appearance of Talos might have the opposite effect. Scaring him into oblivion for another twenty years. There has to be another way.

An idea hits me.

I summon the single flame.

11.

I feel the familiar rushing sensation... and find myself in my living room.

"Oh, hi, Ms. Moon," says a groggy Kai, smiling.

"Hi, Kai. I need my daughter."

"By all means."

He sits up, the blanket falling away from his lanky form. His pointy ears are obvious, ears he can magically "round" quickly whenever necessary. It's a sort of cloaking magic that all elves have.

"Huh, what?" says Tammy, sitting up next to him. She rubs her eyes. "Mom?"

"I need your help, kiddo."

"But we didn't do anything," she says groggily. "Just sleeping."

"I didn't say you did. I said I need your help."

"My help?" she asks, and tries to curl her body around Kai.

But I sit next to her and keep her upright.

"Yes, your help. Now get dressed."

"I am dressed, mama."

"You're in sweats. Actually, that's fine. No one is going to see you."

She blinks a little harder. Wakes up a little more. "Wait, what?"

"We'll be back soon, Kai," I say.

He smiles brightly. But my daughter gasps. "Back?"

Except I've already summoned the single flame, and within it is the cement path and grass, and something massive and glowing...

12.

"Mother!"

Tammy crosses her arms as an admittedly cold blast of air hits us. To my eyes, the place is lit up, especially with the behemoth burning like a mini sun in front of me, as it's now fully in the grass and waddling ever closer to its stopping point. To Tammy's eyes, we're standing in semi-darkness, as only a handful of the park's lights remain on.

"Can you see it?" I ask. I rapidly slip out of my sweater and wrap it around my daughter.

"See what? An empty park? Where are we?"

"No time to explain. Search my thoughts. See what I see. Hurry, hurry!"

"Sheesh! What's your prob—oh, my god."

"You see it?"

"Yes. Unbelievable. It's standing right here?"

"Not exactly. It's walking slowly."

My daughter looks up. I see no light reflecting in her eyes, nothing to indicate a mass of energy is presently glowing in front of her... though in a different spectrum of light completely.

"Mother, it's huge. Is it a dinosaur?"

"I think so."

"What kind?"

"A brontosaurus, I think. Look, we have only minutes before it finishes this cycle, or whatever. It's going to disappear, and it may not come back for another twenty years."

"How do you know this?"

"I would say scan my thoughts, but we don't have time. Tam, I brought you here for a reason."

"You want me to read its mind."

"Actually, I want you to help me communicate with it."

She stares at me blankly. "Mom... this thing has been dead for, what, a billion years or something?"

"Probably closer to a hundred million, and I need you to try. I need you to focus with everything you have."

"But why?"

"I want to help it."

"But why?"

"Tammy! Focus!"

"Sorry, sorry. Okay, hold on. Do you know how stupid I feel trying to talk to a dinosaur?"

"Tammy," I growl under my breath.

"Fine, hold on. Is it right in front of me?"

"More or less. It's moved into the grass. Coming directly at us. Do you see the bloody prints in the grass?"

"Oh, yes. Gross. Okay, at least I know where to focus."

"Use what I see to help you."

"Trust me, I am. Remember, I was sound asleep like two minutes ago."

She faces what she cannot see, but which she knows is there. My seventeen-year-old daughter standing before a ghost dinosaur in the middle of the night in a mostly desolate park. Yeah, it takes a little courage. Then again, she also has me by her side.

"I'm not getting anything, ma."

"Try harder."

"Mom, it's impossible... wait."

I wait, albeit impatiently.

"Never mind. Thought I felt something... wait, hold on."

I hold on as best as I can, knowing this thing is getting ever closer to its cosmic drop off point.

"Got it! It feels pain, mama. Its whole body hurts. It's being swarmed by dozens of hungry things. So many sharp claws, sharp teeth, nowhere to run, so weak..."

Poor thing has been reliving its death, over and over and over again. "Tammy, is it aware of its surroundings at all?"

"Sort of, it's looking for a place to run. It thinks that spot in the grass is a lagoon or something. It's trying to flee to the water. There's just so many..."

Indeed, more and more wounds are opening up on the creature. All told, maybe a hundred bite marks now appear on the big guy. It's also noticeably slowing, staggering almost.

"It doesn't see you, ma. It only sees a pool of dark water. He's so hurt, bleeding everywhere... dying."

The dino stumbles to the side, pauses, sways. Its head reaches down in an act of flinging off the little assassins. More wounds appear on his side. More and more. All running with blood. His light body flashes, briefly disappearing, then returns, now much fainter.

We're losing him.

"Sweetie, can you loop me in to your connection with him?"

"Um, yeah. You want to see what I can see?"

"Yes."

She does so, and my body veritably crawls with pain. She's not so much linked in, as emotionally connected, which might serve me well. Reaching through the pathway created by my daughter, I find myself somewhere close to its mind. "Mind" is not the right word here. Mind and memory would be closer. A memory storehouse. Yet, something is controlling all of this. It is within this loosey-goosey collection of memories that I find myself in.

In it, I see its once pleasant day turn horrifically bad. In it, I see the biting, snapping dinosaurs eating him as he stumbles away. And yes, there is the blackish pond to which it has pinned all its hopes.

I close my eyes and speak directly into its mind, or what's left of it. I tell it over and over again to stop, that it is no longer under attack, that all is well, that it doesn't need to bleed and die and repeat.

"Try images, mother," says Tammy in my head.

I do, going through the same mantra, but

without words, doing my best to conjure images of safety, peace, ease and rest. I show it images of sitting peacefully in the grass. Of its body healing.

With human beings, I can sink into a physical mind, and take hold of thoughts and memories, and change and alter at will. But here, there's nothing to grasp onto, and all I can do is offer suggestions, alternatives. After all, it's not dying right now. It's just reliving the memory.

And so, I try to give it an alternative memory, forming the images as clearly as I can, doing my best to stamp them into its fragmented mind.

It stumbles again, flickering more and more. But something else seems to be happening, too... the wounds along its flanks are disappearing.

"Whoa, Mom! I think it's working!"

It takes another halting step, now so much dimmer. Its head sweeps to the left and right, looking for what it can no longer see. After all, I have given it the image of total health, total peace.

I push for more, though... I push for it to sit down in the grass with me.

But sitting down is not an easy process for the big fella. It takes a series of hitches and shudders, of trying it first this way, then that way, then settles on dropping down on its front elbows, much like a camel. As it does so, I sense my daughter smiling. I remind her to hold our connection, and she does.

I wait for the hind legs to drop down, as the bulk of its light body settles onto the grass of Santana Park, though not a blade seems affected. It lowers its head all the way to the grass, and as it does so, some of the creature's brightness returns.

Now I show him a picture of a tiny female humanoid standing in front of it. My daughter has elected to stay on the cement path, maybe twenty yards away. I project an image of me petting it on the nose, trying like hell to convey a sense of helping it.

"Offer it food, mom."

And so I do, remembering the giant leaves in its memory. I mentally project one such leaf, and lo! The creature on the grass before me mimics eating the giant leaf. I give it maybe a dozen more leafy projections and it mimics eating each one.

I also sense within it... confusion. But also peace. So much peace. It wants to sleep. It wants to close its eyes and sleep forever. It's also curious about the little creature in front of it. It likes when I feed it and pet its nose, which

I am doing now. I give it the suggestion that my touch is warm and relaxing.

Easing myself down before it, the creature rests its mammoth head in my lap. Luckily, there's no actual weight, and I have a sense of being surrounded by white light. I scoot back a smidge and continue petting its snout. Its big, round eye stares at me, then begins to close with each stroke of my hand. Finally, it closes altogether, and a powerful snort of air erupts from its nostrils. Air billows out, though I feel nothing.

"He's going home, Mom. It's happening."

Just as she says the words, the light around me shimmers and fades, and within seconds, the dinosaur is gone. I only just met the big guy, but already I miss him.

"You're crying, ma?"

"Your mom is an old softy."

I sit there for a while longer, wondering where he went, and if he is going to be given more big leafy meals, and if there is someone waiting for him up there who will pet his big snout.

I don't know, but I want to think it is true.

Goodbye, big fella.

The End

Vampire Widow

"You're hearing a voice from the Mojave Desert?"

"I think so, yes."

"Tam, that's like a hundred miles away."

"I know, ma. But it's just coming through so clearly. I think whoever is sending it is also telepathic."

"You don't know who's sending it?"

"She's too far away. I can only hear her voice. If she was closer, I could see into her mind."

"What exactly is she saying?"

"She's asking for help from anyone who can hear her. But mom, it's weird... she's speaking with emotions, and pictures. Not actual words."

"How do you know she's asking for help?"

"It's a feeling I'm getting. Almost like... I'm translating her emotions and pictures into English."

"So, she speaks another language?"

"Maybe. Well, are we going to help this lady or not?"

"It's the middle of the night, Tam."

"When has that stopped you before?"

"Almost never."

"It's going to take us a few hours to get there. Unless I summon Talos."

"No, I think we need to drive. I need to, um, hone in on her. Talos flies too fast and high."

"Then I guess we should go. Let me get dressed."

"Can we get coffee on the way?"

"I might need more than coffee, if you know what I mean."

"Oh, I know. Trust me. The Starbucks on Raymond is open twenty-four hours."

"We'll go there first... then the Mojave desert. Did I really just say that?"

"You did, ma. Think of it as an adventure!"

***

"Uh oh. There are only four people here, including the workers. Will they be enough?"

"Enough to hold me for a few hours."

"But don't take too much, ma. They look tired enough as it is."

"Gee, if only there was a black, hot and delicious liquid for that..."

"Ha ha."

"Trust me, I wish coffee worked on me. Okay, here goes..."

"Whoa! They all yawned in unison! So weird."

"But better than *sucking their blood*, right?"

"Ugh, you do the worst Dracula impressions."

"Trust me, he doesn't sound anything like he does in the movies. Now, what are you having?"

"Mocha latte, duh. But let's wait a sec. The guy behind the register is still yawning..."

"Oopsie."

***

"Can you still hear her?"

"Of course I can still hear her. Tell you what... when I *don't* hear her, I'll tell you. Cool?"

"Cool."

"If anything, her voice is getting stronger."

"And she's still asking for help?"

"Begging for help."

"Begging?"

"Yes—whoa, ma! You're going over ninety!"

"Just keep a look out for police."

"Can't you just erase their memory?"

"I can, but stopping and dealing with them will take up valuable time."

"Oh, right."

"You're going over a hundred! Just remember, you have precious cargo in this car... me!"

"You're adorable. Cat-like reflexes, remember? Now, hang on."

***

"Slow down a little, ma."

"Why? Police ahead?"

"No, you're just going too fast. It's kind of freaking me out. Having a hard time focusing on the distress call."

"Better?"

"Yes, better."

"The turn-off to the desert is coming up, Tammy."

"Where will it take us?"

"That way."

"Yes, take the turn-off. She's coming in stronger. Whoa! She's picking up on me now, too."

"Really? Can you ask her—"

"Hold on, Mom. We're talking now."

***

"You back?"

"I'm back."

"What did she say?"

"Mom... you're not going to believe this."

"Sweetie, we pretty much say that every day of our lives."

"I know... but you really, really aren't going to believe this one."

"That bad?"

"No, that *weird*."

"Okay, hit me..."

***

"You're right, I don't believe it."

"I think she's telling the truth, ma."

"How is it that you can even communicate with her?"

"She's like really old, and really magical."

"This has to be a hoax. 'Fake News' and all that."

"I don't think so, ma. She needs our help, bad."

"Are we really doing this?"

"We really are. And ma?"

"Yeah?"

"Hurry!"

***

"Pull over here."

"To the side of the road?"

"No, wait. Hmm. Go down a little more. See that dirt road?"

"Sweetie, it's all dirt out here."

"I know, but there's an actual road there, according to Google Maps."

"Okay, I see it."

"Go down it."

"For how long?"

"I don't know. Maybe like a mile or two. I'll know when we get a little closer."

"You do know we're in the Momvan, right?"

"I know. And when are you going to finally upgrade? You can buy yourself something nice now. You don't have to drive this old thing."

"This old thing has a lot of memories."

"Yeah, I guess so."

"Besides, it's going to be yours someday soon."

"Oh, god, no."

"Oh, god, yes!"

"Will you just hurry, ma?"

***

"Stop here."

"There's nothing out here, sweetie."

"Well, duh. Their lair is beneath us. They

live underground, obviously. Not a lot of them, but like a hundred or so."

"There are a hundred giant spiders beneath us now?"

"Oh, yes. Maybe more."

"How big are we talking?"

"Like the size of, I dunno, an elephant or something."

"And they called to humans for help?"

"No, she called to others of her kind for help. I just happened to hear her."

"Spiders speak telepathically?"

"Yes. Many animals can."

"I didn't know that."

"Well, it's not something I talk about."

"But spiders...?"

"These aren't just any spiders, Mom. They're kind of like old nature spirits. Like they were worshiped once, long ago."

"Ah, they were created by belief, summoned into existence."

"Yes, but a real long time ago. I know this all sounds crazy and stuff, but she needs help right now. She is about to die. There's been a cave-in. The others can't reach her. She's trapped and so is her egg."

"I assume a giant spider egg?"

"Well, duh. I told her you are not like other humans. You are stronger and can teleport her away from danger, if you can find her. I told her you have the unique ability to see through things for a short distance."

"Like twenty feet."

"Hopefully she's not that far down. The place is riddled with caverns and tunnels."

"And giant spiders."

"Of course."

"I might never stop having the heebee-jeebees."

"She's suffocating, and her babies will die, too. Mom, she's holding up an entire cave-in."

"Okay, let's save a giant spider goddess and her babies. And did I really just say that?"

"You did, and yay!"

***

"Here, ma. She's coming through strongest directly below this spot. But she's getting weaker. She's suffocating."

"Okay, yeah, there's an opening about ten feet under us."

"Do you see her?"

"Not yet. Lots of dust."

"She should be directly under us."

"Trade spots with me. Okay... I see a pile of rocks. Some movement. There's something in those piles of rocks. Something big and black and covered in hair."

"That's her. Can you help her?"

"Maybe. Hang on."

"Where are you going?"

"Scoping out the place. I need to see my landing point option. Hey, I don't see her egg."

"She's hovering over it, Mom. She's literally keeping the rocks off the egg all by herself."

"She's a good mama. Oh, wow!"

"What?"

"I see the rest of them. The spiders, I mean. Dozens of them. The pile of rocks is blocking them from helping her. I think."

"Mom, she can't breathe and she's weakening. She just wants to save her babies. She doesn't care about herself."

"Like I said, a good mama. Okay, I got the lay of the land. I'm ready."

"For what?"

"This."

***

You disappeared, mom.

I'm with her. Does she know who I am?

She knows you're there to help.

Not a lot of room. Luckily, I don't need to breathe.

Well, she's not so lucky.

I know. Ask her where her egg is. I'll try to save it first.

She says it's directly under her.

I see it. Wow, it's a big sucker. And it looks like she's holding up a few tons of rocks and dirt on her shoulders. There's a space under her... teleporting now. Tell her not to move.

She wants to know if that's a joke.

An unintentionally bad joke. There... under her now. Jesus, she's big. And, holy smokes.

What?

You never said she was the world's biggest black widow.

Does it matter?

Probably not. Okay, got the egg. There, done! It's in another part of the cavern.

She says thank you, mom! She senses her babies are safe. She says she can die happy now.

Well, no one is dying on my shift. Tell her to hang on. I'm coming for her next, though I've never teleported anything as big as her.

Just try, ma—whoa! The whole ground shook!

That's the ground caving in. She's been holding it up all by herself.

So she's safe?

She's with her egg... and the others are arriving too. Wow, I've never been happy and creeped out all at once. She just bowed her head.

She's thanking you, Mom.

Tell her it's my pleasure. Returning now.

***

"You're crying, sweetie. Why?"

"I dunno. I just felt her fear and worry for so long, like for the past two or three hours. I'm just so relieved for her. Thank you for helping."

"Hey, she did all the work. And you were the one who led me to her. My job was the easy part."

"Still, she is so relieved. Ma... there's some sort of chanting down there, buzzing. I think it's their way of singing."

"Singing spiders. Now, I've heard of everything. You hungry? I saw some giant flies down there."

"Oh, gross."

"Or we can have some pancakes. There's a cafe down the highway."

"I vote pancakes. Hey, what's wrong?"

"Just thinking about what a good kid you are, Tam Tam."

"Now you're crying!"

"Must be some dust in my eye. This is the desert, after all."

"You can't fool me, mama."
"No, I can't. Let's go, kiddo."

The End

Moon Maze

"I have a question, if that's okay?" says the voice of a young man on the phone.

"Fire away," says the voice of a psychic vampire. No, I don't usually refer to myself in the third person, but there's a first for everything.

"Um, is it true that I can hire you to look into, like... anything?"

"True enough. Whether or not I accept the job is the rub."

"Right, okay. Well, this might be kind of a weird thing to ask a private investigator..."

"Okay, now you're making me nervous."

"I know, sorry, sorry. Okay, here goes... I want you to investigate something I saw a long time ago, something I've always questioned."

"I've gone from nervous to intrigued," I say. "What do you think you saw a long time ago?"

He clears his throat. "I've never told this to anyone except my mom."

"Well, I'm a mom, too. So, fire away."

He chuckles a little. "Okay, so when I was like in kindergarten, I saw something on the side of the road that I don't think I was meant to see."

He explains further. He and his mom were driving to school. They lived in Yorba Linda out near Carbon Canyon at the time, which so happens to be the canyon behind Kingsley's mansion. He had been looking off to the side of the road when he saw a man—or what he thought was a man—appear out of the woods. In one swift motion, the man reached down and pulled open a steel door in the ground, jumped inside, and closed the door on top of him.

"What did you mean by 'you thought was a man'?"

"Well, the man was covered in fur."

"And this was in the morning?"

"No, it was night."

"I thought you were going to school."

"I was. When I asked my mom about it recently, she said we had been going to a parent-teacher conference at school. I'd forgotten that part. I just knew I had been on my way to school."

"Did she remember you mentioning the hairy man?"

"She did, yes."

"Did she see him?"

"No, but she remembers me making a fuss over it. Which kind of proves I didn't make the whole night up."

"But it also doesn't mean you saw what you think you saw. How dark was it?"

"Not full dark. I saw the guy pretty clearly."

"Dusk?"

"Yes, dusk," he says, seemingly trying the word on for size for the first time. "My mom said something else."

"Go on."

"She said I called him an apeman."

"Makes sense, you saw him covered in fur."

"Yes. But I was only like five or six at the time. I wasn't sure what I was seeing then."

"And you're sure now?"

"I am."

"Okay. So what did you see?"

"The devil."

***

"Well, it wasn't me," says Kingsley. "Despite Carbon Canyon being directly behind my house. Didn't he say the thing had horns?"

"Yes. But it was also covered in fur."

"Well, only half right."

We're sitting together on an outside couch, under his patio cover. A fire roaring in a nearby brick fireplace. Orchestral music plays over his hidden speakers. We're snuggling like pros.

"I understand that. But what I don't understand is why you have a full living room outdoors."

"Because it beats lawn chairs and sitting around a campfire."

"But does it?"

"I have ten acres behind me for lawn chairs and fire pits. Think of this as an extension of the house."

"A house that's already nearly 10,000 feet."

"What can I say, Sammy? I make a lot of money and I like nice things."

"Not complaining. Just trying to understand the man behind all this outdoor wicker."

"The man behind it sometimes doesn't know what to do with all his money."

"Donate it?"

"I do. In droves."

I sip from my wine glass. Haven't been buzzed in over a decade—well, not by wine—but I still like the taste of it. "Where did you make all your money?"

"The house before this one, mostly. I sold it for nineteen million. Work as a defense attorney has been lucrative at best. I have stock, bonds, investments around the world." He takes a pull from his can of Miller Lite. For a guy who likes the finer things in life, his beer needs are as base as they get. "How old was the kid again when he saw this thing in the woods?"

"He says five or six. About fifteen years ago. Were you here fifteen years ago?"

"I was."

"Do you recall ever getting loose and finding your way down through an opening at the side of the road?"

"I do not, though my memory is sketchy when I turn. That said, I am usually aware of when I have escaped. The entity in me is pleased and seeks destruction."

"If it wasn't you fifteen years ago, who was it then?"

"Sam, as you well know, I'm not the only werewolf in Orange County."

It's a nice night out. Autumn coolness in the air. Hardly a reason to have the fireplace going, but Kingsley likes to set a mood. I note his barefoot is exactly two and a half times the size of my barefoot.

"You get pedicures?" I ask him.

"I do. One of the great joys in life is having one's feet and toes attended to."

"Are you sure you're a fierce creature of the night?"

"Just the one night."

"Have you ever heard of anyone taking cover inside of one of those side-of-the-road steel doors?"

"No."

"You know the ones I'm talking about right?"

Kingsley nods. "Steel doors, maybe aluminum. Steel might be too heavy. Usually double doors, almost like trap doors into the ground."

"Yeah. What are they for?"

"Electricians, most likely."

"Big enough for a werewolf with horns?"

"It likely wasn't a werewolf, Sam. Remember, when we turn, most of us are out of our minds with rage. Trust me, when I turn each month, I'm not running through the forest looking for double doors to hide inside. I'm looking, quite frankly, for corpses."

"My boyfriend, folks."

"Hey, I'm a good catch for twenty-nine nights of the months. The thirtieth... not so much."

I pat his hand, noting the tuft of fur-like hair at the back of it. He raises a remote control, pushes a button, and a flatscreen TV rises up from an entertainment center in front of us. "Should we start the movie now?"

"Or," I say, "we can go find that glorified manhole."

"You say the sweetest things, my love."

***

Find it, we do.

Kingsley pulls off the side of the road, deep into the bushes, scratching the hell out of his Lincoln Navigator and not seeming to care that he has. He shrugs, says, "Franklin and the boys can buff it out."

Franklin and the boys being, of course, his small collection of Lichtenstein monsters who live in his expansive basement, and treat him as their god-like master. Yeah, kind of revolting, but he can't do anything about it.

I take in the cool air and scan the wooded surroundings. Years ago, I once heard of a councilman crashing his car nearby here. Ended up with a broken arm and other injuries. Found his Cadillac in a creek. Always wondered how he ended up in a creek, so far off the road. Did it have something to do with werewolves? Or something else?

"You're sure this is the one?" asks Kingsley.

I am sure. The kid spent the next few years passing the opening on his way to school. Says he stared at it every day but never saw anyone or anything near it again. He'd texted me a screenshot of Google Maps, along with the coordinates.

Speaking of school, I need to enroll Paxton in junior high. Paxton being, of course, the girl

I'd recently adopted... a girl who, at present, used my office as her bedroom. With Anthony going away soon to Light Warrior school, his bedroom would be available to her. For now, though, I worked at the kitchen table.

Three kids. Yeah, wow. All of it is still so new, so crazy, so *trying* at times. But Anthony and Tammy have made Paxton feel welcomed, and seeing the three of them bond has been the highlight of my life these past few months.

Focus, Sam.

As the crow flies, we are maybe five miles from Kingsley's backyard. That's a lot of empty space for southern California. And a great place to hunt deer, too. Though Franklin usually does the hunting, often weeks before the full moon... definitely long enough for the body to putrefy nicely for Kingsley's sophisticated pallet.

A decade ago, I'd spent a little time out here as well, teaching a lesson to a crime boss who had managed to down a plane full of witnesses. Pretty sure he didn't make it out alive. Not by my hand, granted. But by the hands of those he'd harmed; in particular, their families. Helluva lesson.

But that showdown of sorts had been a few miles away. And back then, I hadn't noticed the two-door manhole cover off to the side of the road. Truthfully, I think few do. They're sort of there, in the background. Trapdoors into the earth that few of us think about.

The question is: can I trust a young boy's memory? I don't know, but I believe his story, even though I didn't have access to his mind at the time. Unlike my daughter, my telepathic charms only work so far... not dozens of miles over the phone line.

Why else would he hire me, unless he believed his own story? True, this could be a practical joke... but one that cost him $50. Yes, I'd charged him a $50 retainer fee to see how serious he'd been. Sure enough, he'd sent me the payment via PayPal, and I was officially on the case. When I called him back, I could veritably hear the glee in his voice. I told him I would give him a full report the next day, which would be tomorrow. I imagined him grinning ear to ear by the time we hung up.

I kinda am too. After all, it isn't everyday one is hired to look into the mother of all creepy manhole covers... or whatever this is called.

Once officially on the job, I tried doing a search on such covers and could find nothing that wasn't attached with an Amazon, Lowe's or Home Depot ad. As far as I can tell, Kingsley might be right. These things could be associated with underground electrical cables. But that had been as far as I got before heading out to Kingsley's place for a dinner date. After all, he'd been marinating steaks for the past two days. Since I got no nutritional value out of them, I suspect the steaks were more for him, than me.

Kingsley looks at me from across the front seat. "We counted, what, five such openings on the way out here?"

"We did," I say.

"I had no idea so many were around. I mean they just sort of blend into the background."

"That they do. Trap doors into a subterranean world none of us question."

We step out of the Navigator and shut both doors with just enough *oomph* to click shut, but not loud enough to draw too much attention. Then again, if we were dealing with something supernatural, it could likely hear us; that is, of course, if it was *above* ground.

Being an alternate route out of Orange County makes this road popular for motorists seeking a respite from the freeways... that is, until this road becomes nearly as congested. Last time I tried it, I might have saved maybe five minutes. Kind of not worth it... unless you account for the pretty nature drive one gets out of the deal. Luckily, my work doesn't include too many trips into Riverside County during the evening rush hour.

For now, the road is empty. And few would

spot the black Navigator in the bushes anyway. We have the place to ourselves. I lead the way over to the double doors set in the ground.

"This is it, according to the coordinates." I kick some debris away from the metal doors, lean down and read the writing imprinted on the left flap. "You're right. This one says 'Electrical.'"

"I'm smarter than I look," says Kingsley.

I squat down. "What do you make of these recessed loops?"

He takes a knee and runs a thick finger over them. "Looks to me like a special tool is needed, one that slips down and releases the hooks."

"So how does a full-on werewolf come out of the woods and open one of these doors?"

"Because it wasn't a werewolf, Sam," says Kingsley. "We might have varying degrees of crazy, but I doubt any of us are coherent enough to use a tool to unlock these doors."

"But it's possible some are decidedly less crazy than you and Mazarak?"

Kingsley nods. "Yeah, we are pretty far off on the crazy scale. Honestly, when that bastard takes over, I just slink into a dark corner of my mind, cover my ears, and wait for the blessed morning light. I've even caught myself singing Christmas songs. Anything to block the crazy

I'm witnessing."

"So you have no control over him?"

"Just about none. I suppose I could come out of the shadows and do my best to talk sense into him, as I had done all those years ago when he broke into your hotel room. But it's like arguing with a rabid dog."

"What's his deal?"

"My best guess, he went insane during the whole dark masters training. I suspect he was murdered by his fellow practitioners. Something like that."

"Is he listening to us now?"

"Hmm. Not really. He's in the background, pacing in the shadows, talking to himself in a language I don't understand. He wants to kill something."

"Any chance he can get over his issues someday?"

"Hard to say. He's been like this for the last fifty years."

"Hmm. But maybe not all are as insane as him?"

"I hope not, but many are pretty messed up."

"Well, fifteen years ago, something not-so-insane pried this door up without damaging it. Which means, it had a tool of some sort."

"Which means, it often used these doors."

I nod. "If it does, maybe the tool is around

here somewhere."

"Or we can just have you peek through the doors and tell us what's inside."

"Not a bad idea. But wouldn't it be more fun if we discovered it together by opening these flap thingies?"

"Um, no."

"Fine, hold on."

I take a deep breath... and project my thoughts down through the metal doors and into a small space. I describe what I see: "There's a recessed space there. Big enough for two men, or one Kingsley."

"Ha ha."

"There are tubes of wires passing along one side of the opening, and a control panel, along with a small shelf or desk."

"I'm guessing the electricians plug in their laptops or equipment there."

"One of the tubes turns and heads north under the road and goes that way." I point over my shoulder without shifting my focus from the small chamber.

"Hmm," says Kingsley. "There's a house out there, maybe a quarter mile away, up on the hill. This must also serve as a relay for that house. See anything else? Maybe push beyond the cement chamber?"

"Pushing now."

"Push it real good, Sam."

Without looking, I reach out and smack him. From the sound of it, I got his meaty shoulder. Might as well have slapped the side of a mountain.

"Bingo," I say.

"What does 'bingo' mean?"

"It means there's a man-made tunnel behind the south wall. A slab of cement conceals it. The tunnel goes south, away from the street and into the canyon. And that's all I've got. I've reached the end of my range."

"The tunnel isn't cement? With wires or anything?"

"Nope. Kind of looks like an old mining shaft."

I blink and come back into my body... and stumble a bit. Kingsley's prepared for this and holds on to me.

"Well, that kind of proves the kid's point," he says. "Something is or was using this as a tunnel entrance. Possibly as a tunnel exit, too. What were the parameters of your assignment?"

"To back up his claim that he saw something come out of the woods and disappear down through these doors."

"The evidence of the tunnels should back up his claim nicely. How big was the tunnel?"

"Big enough for you to walk through. So it's

—"

"Don't say it, Sam."

"Ginormous."

"Oh, brother. Yes, I'm big. Yes, I'm hairy. Yes, I'm a great lover. Can we quit pointing out the obvious and move on... and go home?"

I snicker. "I'm giving you that last one only because it's true."

"Thank you... now let's get the hell out of —"

"We're not going anywhere, big guy. Not until we figure out who's using these tunnels and why."

"The *why* wasn't part of your parameters, Sam."

"They are now."

He exhales. "I was afraid you were going to say that."

"Quit your moaning, fella. The game's afoot!"

"You mean, the mystery's underfoot."

"That too!"

"Why are you yelling?"

"I dunno. But this is kinda fun, don't you think?"

"If you say so, Sammy. So what now?"

"Now, we go into the tunnel, of course."

"Okay, I was *really* afraid you were going to say that. Can't we just follow the tunnel above ground, while you scan below?"

I shake my head. "Can't really move and scan. I get too dizzy, and we would move far too slow. Faster to just be in the tunnel. Besides, I'm pretty sure the tunnel angles *down*. Meaning, below my scanning range."

"How much did the kid pay you to help him?"

"Fifty bucks."

"I'll pay you five thousand to forget all this and go home and snuggle with me."

"I reject your offer. Well, for now. There will be snuggling to be had in the near future."

"Fine. Then let's open this thing. You want to smash it or me?"

I shake my head. "Probably not a good idea to alert whoever uses this trap door that we know about it. Plus, the city still uses this. Any damage to it would alert them, too, and might give them cause to investigate further. God only knows what's down in that tunnel. That said, there's probably a tool around here somewhere."

We split up, but it doesn't take long for me to find the rod-like tool with a hooked end in the cobwebby opening of a nearby tree. I might be immortal, but it gives me the willies when I stick my hand inside that hollowed opening. I shiver, run in place a little, and veritably throw it at Kingsley. He snatches it, shakes his head sadly at me, studies it. Nods as if he understands what he's looking at, then moves over to the ground-level doors. He slips the rounded end inside an opening, hooks one of the recessed loops within, and pulls. Sure enough, two handholds pop up. Kingsley and I each grab hold of one and pull a door. We repeat the action on the opposite door, and soon, both are wide open in the night.

"Easy-peasy," he says.

"Then why are you sweating?"

"Because I weigh nearly three hundred and fifty pounds and I'm covered with hair."

"You really weigh that much?"

"Sam, I'm nearly six foot eight, and covered in muscle."

"Umm..."

"Along with a comfortable layer of insulation."

"That's one way to say it."

"Hey, my kind aren't necessarily known for staying lean. That said, even I've noticed I'm bigger than usual."

"Does that mean...?"

"Yes, I'm due for a growth spurt."

"How much of a spurt?"

He shrugs. "Probably a quarter of an inch."

"And how often do these spurts happen

again?"

"Once every few years."

"Is it safe to say you grow an inch every... decade?"

"It's safe. But it does seem to be slowing down a bit. I think there's a ceiling as to how tall I'll get."

I nod. "Stands to reason. The bigger you are, the more attention you attract."

"A balance of being tall, but not too tall."

"All of which makes your monthly transitions easier and less painful?"

"Exactly."

"How tall is it?"

"The wolfman?" he asks.

"Yes."

"I dunno. You tell me. You saw him."

"Your head went up to the ceiling in the hotel room... a ceiling that had to be at least ten feet high."

"There you go."

"How tall do you think you'll get?"

"No clue, Sam. My guess is maybe around seven feet, maybe a little taller." He motions to the dark maw in the ground. "You ready to go exploring?"

"Let's do this."

***

The squarish opening that drops down is about six feet.

There's a metal stepladder attached to the wall, and more cobwebs than I care to deal with, but I guess that's proof this opening hasn't been used for a while. I drop down first because I fit better, and scan the south-facing cement wall, all too aware of a black widow spider just a foot away from my face. I send a mental projection for it to scram, and it does, veritably tripping over its eight legs to get the hell out of there. Thanks to none other than Dracula, I learned to control animals... even insects. I don't use such control often, but in the case of a spider in front of my face... um, yeah.

"I don't see anything here to open the wall."

"Try pushing it on the side. Might be a pivot system in place," suggests Kingsley.

"And who the hell would have made a pivoting cement wall?"

"My guess is whoever built the tunnel."

I'm about to put some weight behind one side of the wall, when my phone pings.

"Who's that?" asks Kingsley.

I fish the phone out my back pocket. "It's a text from my client."

"He texts you at two in the morning?"

"I told him I was a night owl, that he could

text me any time."

"You *used* to be a night owl," says Kingsley.

I shrug. "Old habits die hard."

"Fine, what does he say?"

"It's a date."

"He asked you out on a date?"

"No, silly. It's the date of his parent-teacher conference from fifteen years ago. I asked him to look into it."

"I take it you didn't tell him why."

"Nope. Hold on."

"What are you doing?"

"Plugging the date into my full moon app. Told you it would come in handy. Okay, whoa."

"Whoa, what?"

"It wasn't a full moon on that night."

"Hmm... so it wasn't a wolfman he saw disappear into this tunnel."

"Appears not," I say. "Remember, he thought it had been an apeman at first."

"At first? What did he think it was later?"

"The devil."

"Wow, that just did the impossible," says Kingsley.

"Oh, what's that?"

"That creeped even me out. You sure you want to go through with this?" he asks.

"More so than ever."

Kingsley is right. The south wall pivots in

the center, though no mortal human could have moved it. Heck, I barely budge it. It takes both of us pushing together to open it enough to squeeze through. Full disclosure... Kingsley does all the squeezing.

"Hang on," I say, and dash back out and pull the metal doors down. We next shut the cement wall behind us.

"Great," says Kingsley, his eyes shining yellow. "Now we're sealed in."

"Where's your sense of adventure?"

"Back home. Under the sheets."

"Since when did you become such an old man?"

"I'm nearly ninety years old, Sam."

"Except you're gonna live to like three thousand years. So, really, you're just a big hairy kid in the grand scheme of things. Emphasis on the big and hairy."

"Are you quite done?"

I hold up a finger. "Almost."

"What is it?"

"Hold on. Wow, okay. Just got a psychic hit of a man building this secret doorway. A human male with exceptional strength."

"Well, someone had to build it. Is there something else?"

I wait as an image tries to form in my mind. Interestingly, these psychic nudges started happening with the ejection of Elizabeth. Allison thinks the highly evolved dark master had blocked my connection to the natural world. With her now gone, I can once again practice witchcraft... and receive psychic help.

"Okay, yeah. I'm pretty sure I just saw the man shift... into something massive."

"So we are dealing with a shape-shifter."

"I think so."

"Well, I guess it takes a shifter to find a shifter. Let's go."

***

We make our way through what I am certain is complete darkness. Then again, I never know when its complete darkness anymore. For me, the world is continuously illuminated in shimmering white light particles.

Meanwhile, the tunnel is wide enough for us to walk side by side, which we do, until I eventually take the lead. At one point, I pause and project my thoughts upward... and see only dirt. Yup, we are definitely angling down.

"Who do you think made this tunnel?" I ask.

"Whatever that kid saw, maybe. Or, more likely, this is part of an old mine shaft."

"There are mines here?"

"Indeed. Hundreds of them, in fact. All off

the beaten track, of course. Gold and silver mostly. No one ever really hit the mother-lode, and so the mines came and went without much fanfare. But the miners sure as hell tried to strike it rich out here. Carbon Canyon is riddled with such systems. Franklin and I see them everywhere."

"Let me guess, when you're hunting deer."

"But of course. And I heard that tone."

"I didn't have a tone."

"You had a little tone. You don't approve of my monthly feeding habits. Let me remind you... they're not *my* monthly habits."

"I know. The dark master in you."

"Master is a bit of a reach. The dark psychopath in me."

"Yet he learned enough to escape the devil and the cycle of reincarnation."

"The dark masters attracted all types to their cause, Sam. And not all fair well over time."

"Meaning?"

"Some grow crazier and crueler. Be glad you are free of yours."

"Mazarak does not seek freedom?"

"He enjoys our relationship for now. He also enjoys the life I provide him."

"Even though he's rarely front and center?"

"Once a month is enough for him; at least, for now."

"And he's okay with that?"

"It's hardwired into our make-up, Sam, built upon the legends and belief of the very nature of werewolves. Not to mention, being a shape-shifter fit his personality. Truth is, Mazarak is not equipped to take care of himself. I handle the physical, financial, and social for twenty-nine days out of the month. He relies on me for stability. Of course, had Mazarak been more savvy and sophisticated, and less violent and prone to anger, I would have likely been a vampire. Then again, I, too, had similar wolfen qualities. I was physical, having worked as a fisherman. I was always, ah, naturally hairy. I had a thick beard at a young age, for instance. So yeah, the 'powers that be' determined that a werewolf was the best result."

"Should I ask about the powers that be?"

"Hard to know, Sam. But there is obviously a system in place that helps determine such outcomes. The very nature of creation in this world is at the heart of it. Also, the intent of the dark master, and likely the energy of the victim."

"You had, um, hair energy?"

"I had a wild energy, Sam. I never wanted to be contained. I liked fishing on the open seas, for instance. When I was younger, I enjoyed running free in the forests near my home."

"How does working in a courtroom satisfy that need?"

"It doesn't, not really. I chose the profession because I wanted for once to use my mind, rather than my body. Sam, I've been an attorney for nearly thirty years. I am getting to the point where my colleagues are asking about my youthful appearance. Guys in their thirties are now sixty. And here I am, chugging along, growing bigger and sexier."

I chuckle. He does too.

"You know what I mean, Sam. I am likely going to have to look for a new profession and change my name. Again. Pain in my ass, let me tell you."

"I haven't had to deal with that yet, thank God."

"You've got another ten, fifteen years still. Which way, Sam? Left or right?"

We come across a fork in the tunnel. Both directions look promising.

"I dunno."

"What does your intuition tell you?" he asks.

"Honestly? I don't feel strongly one way or the other. You pick one, big fella."

"Let's go right."

"Then left it is."

He chuckles. "You're too much, Sam Moon."

We go left and ten minutes later we come to another fork. Still no psychic hit, though my inner alarm pings. Just once. Is it an errant ping, or are we making a wrong choice here? And if we are making a wrong choice, then why isn't my newfound extrasensory perception kicking in to help guide the way? I don't know, but I do suspect something strange: it doesn't matter which choice we make. Why I think that, I don't know, but there it is.

Ten minutes later, another fork. We choose the left tunnel and start down it when my inner alarm pings *twice*.

"Hold on," I say, pointing to my head. "Just got another warning."

"Should we try the right tunnel?"

"Couldn't hurt."

Try we do, and my alarm pings twice again. Realizing it doesn't matter which tunnel entrance we choose, we continue down the right... until we come across another fork.

"What the hell? I mean, I know this area is riddled with more mining shafts than people around here even know about, but... why so many side tunnels? And why no indicator to help a miner find his way in or out?"

I shrug. "It's almost like we're being led purposely deeper."

"Or purposely getting lost. Truth is, I think

we might be lost."

"I think we might be, too."

"Should we try to retrace our steps, Sammy?"

"I might have a number of gifts, but a photographic memory isn't one of them." I sigh. "We've made like seven turns at this point."

Kingsley's amber eyes flash. "If you didn't have the ability to teleport us out of here, I might actually start getting a little nervous."

"That's never a pretty sight."

He chuckles. "Does it even matter which tunnel we choose at this point?"

"Probably not."

And so we choose the one on the right, and as soon as we enter it, my inner alarm pings five times. We test the left, and get the same five pings. We continue left.

I am not sure where we are going, but one thing is certain.

We are lost as hell.

***

We pass three more such forks, the last of which is a three-pronged deal.

"The middle?" suggests Kingsley.

We are barely a half dozen steps when the ringing begins in my head, and doesn't let up.

"Should we go back and try another?" he asks.

I shake my head, distracted by the noise going on between my ears. Usually, the ringing either lessens or disappears when all my senses are necessary to stay alive. So, at the moment, the ringing is both a good thing and a bad thing. It lets me know that something is coming, but isn't here yet... whatever the hell it is.

On edge, and willing the sound in my head to lighten up, we continue on until we hit a dead end.

"Well, shit," says Kingsley. "Alarm still sounding?"

"Yup, but not to the point of driving me crazy. Something's here or coming for us."

"You're making me nervous, Sammy."

"Join the club. I almost want whatever it is to get here just so the damn ringing stops."

"Be careful what you wish for."

We scan the surroundings. There's not much to see. Whoever had dug this tunnel simply stopped right here, either purposely creating a dead end, or gave up searching for whatever they were searching for. We are about to turn back, when Kingsley snaps his head up.

"Did you hear that?"

"I heard something, not sure what."

"Sounded like a grunt. Maybe a snort. Like

from a pig or boar."

His hearing is better than mine, so I take his word for it. We take a few steps back the way we came when the ground shakes.

"Earthquake?" I ask.

Kingsley shakes his shaggy head. "Footsteps. Whatever it is, it's coming toward us."

"There," I say. "At the far end of the tunnel."

"You can see it?"

I nod. My night vision has always been a tad better than Kingsley's, which for some reason always bugs him. For now, he keeps his issues to himself. "What's it doing?"

"Just standing there."

"Any idea what it is?"

"Nope," I say. "But it's big. Bigger than both of us combined, I'd say."

"Well, shit."

"You can say that again. No way we're going around it or through it."

"Teleport?"

"If we have to," I say. "Whoa."

"Whoa, what?"

"Something just... hit me."

"Hit you how?"

I shake my head, reach a hand out to stabilize myself. "I don't know. It's like a pulsating wave of... sound. You don't feel it?"

"No, but I heard it, though I wasn't sure *what* I was hearing. Now I think I do."

I struggle to stand upright. "Well... what the hell... is it?"

"I think you are experiencing the effects of something called infrasound, a sort of low-frequency growl used to stun prey. Tigers are known to emit it, along with other apex predators."

"Well, hell," I say. It's all I can do to work my tongue in my mouth. "Is it affecting you?"

"No, but I'm not a prey animal."

"And... I... am?"

"Well, a human would be. A blood vampire, likely would not be. You are something in-between now. Likely, if you were a full human, you wouldn't be able to speak."

I blink, which takes a good two or three seconds. "Is that... thing... a... tiger?"

"No clue. Without any wind, I haven't caught its scent yet. But I can hear it. And in-between the low growls there is a lot of snorting. And by the sounds of it, I'd say it's moving towards us again."

And so it is. I can both feel it, and now hear it. Though to my ears, it still sounds like the low rumble of earth moving, not so much footsteps.

"It's big," I say, squinting forward. I note

my mouth works again.

"We established that. You feeling any better?"

"Yeah... the paralysis feeling is almost gone."

"Likely, it thinks we're stunned."

"Seriously, what the *eff* is it?"

"I don't know, Sammy. But we're about to find out..."

***

"Uh oh," I say.

"What's wrong?"

"I can't summon the flame."

"What flame? Oh, shit. *That* flame?"

"Yes."

I try again. The flame appears, immediately sputters as if in a sharp wind, then disappears. "I think that thing somehow blocked my ability to teleport."

"So, we're stuck?"

"For now."

"Well, shit."

"You can say that again."

"Just caught its scent, Sam."

"And?"

"It's a man and a... hmm."

"What?"

Kingsley shrugs. "A bull."

"The maze..." I say.

"Is really a labyrinth," finishes Kingsley. "I think it's a..."

"Minotaur."

***

"What the hell is a minotaur doing down here?"

"No clue, Sammy."

"And last I checked, bulls eat grass," I say. "Hardly an apex predator."

"This isn't your average bull. The Minotaur in Greek mythology was fed a steady stream of sacrificial victims. To be more precise, young maidens. Luckily, he was killed by Theseus."

"Then who's he?"

"I don't know, but likely, it's closer to something like me."

"A were-bull?"

"Possibly. How and when it shifts is unknown to me. I know mermaids can shift at will. I myself can turn full wolf at will. Wolfman, not so much."

I thought of the psychic hit I'd received earlier, of the man building the secret wall. "I think you're right—wait are you saying there's enough belief in the existence of minotaurs to bring them about?"

"Apparently so."

"But how does this work? Was this guy bitten by another minotaur?"

"Possibly, though not likely."

"What do you mean? And lest we forget he's coming toward us."

"But cautiously. Probably doesn't know what to make of us."

"He's used to his victims being good and stunned by this point?"

Kingsley nods. "I think so. And to answer your question... he might be one of the originals. Perhaps even the first."

"But I thought Thesaurus killed him."

"Theseus. And yeah, he did, according to Greek Mythology. No, I'm talking about the first dark master/human hybrid. If so, then no one bit anyone."

"Immaculate conception?" I ask.

"Something like that."

"Holy smokes, he's big. Look at those shoulders."

"You're supposed to only look at my shoulders."

"Really? Jealous of a bull?"

"Jealousy crosses species. Well, it does when you're a shifter."

"You're being ridiculous. So how did he get

here?"

"Hard to know, Sam. Maybe he shipped himself out here on a freighter a century ago."

"But why here?"

"You'll have to ask him. But the network of forgotten mines might have been appealing."

"And he added to them?"

"Yeah, maybe."

"Perhaps that's what minotaurs do," I say. "They create mazes to confuse victims... then stalk them once they come to a dead end."

"Seems about right."

"Do you think he talks?" I ask.

"I don't think he can, Sam. Not with the head of a bull."

The creature stops, and now I can hear him breathing too. I can also see him quite clearly. It stands nearly to the top of the tall tunnel, which means he's about two feet taller than Kingsley. His horns nearly reach to either side of the tunnel. Its eyes flare red... likely the result of the flame within it. Which means its dark master is regarding us. It balls its hands into fists. Big hands. Human hands. The bull part of him stops at his upper chest; the human part is roped with muscle. I wonder what it does down here. I wonder what it eats. I wonder how long it has been since it last ate, and get a feeling that it might have been a long, long time since its last meal. After all, how many people venture down into these tunnels? Maybe one a year, maybe less. Have the trespassers all been eaten by this guy? I don't know, but this thing could easily kill and eat a lost hiker.

"Can you summon the flame yet, Sammy?"

I shake my head. "Not yet."

After sizing us up, the minotaur moves toward us again, its massive, human legs crashing down over the dirt floor.

"Any ideas?" asks Kingsley. "If so, I'm all ears."

"None—okay maybe one."

"Let's hear it."

"You're not going to like it."

"Sam, what choice do we have? This thing is like two feet taller than me and outweighs me by two hundred pounds—maybe more."

"You done yammering?"

"I am."

"Okay, here's the plan..."

***

Kingsley shakes his head. "Sam, this is uncharted territory."

"So is being pulverized by a minotaur. Hurry, big guy. At least ask him."

"I did, and he says he's not sure he can

appear without the full moon."

"Remind him we're thirty feet or more underground. For all he knows there is a full moon above."

"He says he's tied to the moon cycles and won't stand for your lies."

"Tell him to fuck the moon cycles. He either comes out to play, or we all die. Pretty sure we quit being immortal once we hit the digestive fluids."

"He says you make a compelling argument. He will try."

"Tell him to do more than try. Meanwhile, I'll do my best to slow this asshole down."

With the ejection of Elizabeth from my body, my natural magical abilities have returned, albeit slowly. In fact, I only know a few spells, and one of them is throwing small fireballs. I do this now, launching them down the tunnel, one after another. Though diminutive, they have the effect I was looking for. The thing slows, then stops altogether. One of the fireballs explodes against his chest. He roars and wipes it off... and charges again.

"Where we at, big guy?" I ask over my shoulder, launching more fire.

"We're trying, Sam."

The ground shakes and debris falls from the dirt ceiling. Snorting and growling washes over me. Luckily, not of the infrasound variety.

"Stand back, Sam!"

I leap out of the way as Kingsley rushes past me down the hall. He stops and throws his head and shoulders, jerking and convulsing violently. A moment later, his clothing explodes off him, showering over me. When I snatch his shredded light jacket off my face, there, standing before me, is a nearly-turned wolfman. Nearly. Before my eyes, it grows another foot or two, muscle filling out its shoulders and monstrous thighs. It throws its head back as the last remnants of Kingsley's face morphs into that of the wolfman. Not quite the head of a wolf; truly a combination of the two. It turns its head toward me, hate in its wild amber eyes, then turns toward the rumbling coming from the mine shaft before us.

It lets loose a terrifying roar... and charges forward.

My boyfriend, everyone.

***

Minotaur and wolfman slam into each other with enough force to shake the earthen walls around me. Chunks of ceiling drop and the ground quakes... and there's not a damn thing I can do about it but hope and pray that the tunnel holds up.

The charging bull-man had a lot of momentum behind him, so I'm not surprised to see the minotaur win this first round. The wolfman is forced back. Almost to the point of flailing and stumbling.

Almost.

The big canine digs his clawed paws into the dirt floor... and soon holds his ground. The minotaur roars—mercifully, not one of its subsonic, paralyzing growls—grabs the wolfman by the shoulders and slams him into the wall. Not satisfied, it does so again and again, as more and more dirt clods drop down. Choking dust soon fills the air.

The wolfman manages to get its front claws hooked under his opponent's massive shoulders. From this point of leverage, it slams the minotaur up into the ceiling. Uh oh. Chunks of dirt break free... followed by the mother of all rumbling. Something not very good begins happening all around us.

Mazarak, the name of Kingsley's dark master and who presently has control of the wolfman, seems to realize its critical error, though that did nothing to stop his attack as the wolfman now clamps its jaws around the minotaur's massive neck. Or tries to.

Wrong move. The neck is too thick. Mazarak's jaws can't quite get a firm hold, try as he might.

This only seems to enrage the bull. The creature shakes him off, the force of which hurls Kingsley into the wall, exacerbating the rumbling that now seems to be coming from everywhere at once.

The bull stands and now the two creatures circle each other, even as a legit earthquake seems to overtake the tunnel. Remarkably, the wolfman catches my eye, seemingly all too aware that we are about to be buried alive.

I summon the single flame... and it nearly holds, but flutters gain.

The wolfman seems aware of my limited abilities and does something remarkably smart for a half-insane wolfman... it backs away from the enraged bull. Moving toward me.

Beyond them, I can see the dust cloud forming in the tunnel. And behind the dust cloud, I can see the cause of it. The tunnel is caving in from all sides, and it only seems to be picking up steam.

I try the flame again... it holds, wavers, holds again, then vanishes.

Shit.

The wolfman turns to look at me again, as an unholy rumble fills the tunnel, the minotaur literally bulls his way past him... and charges at me. It all happens in a blink, and the impossibly wide mythical creature soon fills the tunnel before me. True, I could wield the Devil Killer, and likely destroy the thing coming at me. Then again, the Devil Killer will not stop the tunnel that is caving in behind him.

I try the flame one more time—and before it can waver, I visualize the spot just behind the charging bull... and jump.

I appear next to a confused Mazarak, who's already covering his head. Grabbing his elbow, I summon the flame again, and visualize within it the only place I can think of...

Just as the tunnel implodes.

***

We land in Kingsley's jail cell beneath his house, gasping and covered in dirt.

Next to me, the wolfman stumbles, confused, then recognizes his surroundings. It lets loose with a wall-shaking roar and turns to me.

"Who's a good boy?" I ask, and summon the flame.

Mazarak doesn't attack, as I know Kingsley will not allow him to, but he sure as hell has murder in his eyes.

I'm gone before it can act on its rage.

***

An hour later, a robed and disheveled Kingsley appears in his rebuilt kitchen nook. 'Rebuilt' because a few years ago the nook took the brunt of a demon attack.

"Want some coffee?" I ask.

"I'll take the whole pot, thank you very much."

I set the steaming pot in front of the big guy, who guzzles half of it. I know for a fact the coffee is piping hot. Watching Kingsley knock it back, one would never know.

"Still mad at me?" I ask.

"Trying not to be. We didn't have to put ourselves in that position."

"I know. Hard for me to let it go, ya know?"

"I understand, but in this case we probably should have. Nothing was to be gained down there. The beast wasn't harming anyone. There have been no known disappearances in the area in many years. We should have left well enough alone."

"I agree. Which is why I went back and fetched him from under the rubble."

"You did? How did you find him?"

"I needed to only visualize the space where he had last been standing. Believe it or not, there had been a small crawlspace under him.

The big guy had been holding up most of the cave-in around him."

"Unbelievable."

"I teleported him out to one of the offshoots, and got the hell out of there."

"Didn't you do something similar with..."

"A giant spider? Yes. I should add cave-in rescue to my list of services."

"Still, a lot of that was unnecessary, Sam."

"I know," I say. "But you see... here's the thing. I'm going to investigate something like that pretty much every time. I kinda don't know how to let something go."

Kingsley is busy glugging the rest of the coffee, some of which escapes down the corners of his mouth. He sets the pot down and wipes his face with the back of his hand. Crazy as it sounds, he makes the sloppy gesture look good.

"I know that about you, Sam. Trust me. It's just that... ah, screw it. We both made it out alive."

"And now we know we have a minotaur living nearby."

"Not sure what to do with that information."

"Maybe something, maybe nothing. But at least we know where to look in case a hiker disappears nearby. Then again, I could always teleport him to a forgotten island."

Kingsley shakes his head, his robe opening a

little. Kingsley always lets his robe open a little. I think he's a little too impressed with his own hairy chest. "He's not hurting anyone down there."

"How does he eat?"

"Likely animals above ground, which is why your young client saw him running through the brush. Like I said, I haven't heard of too many hikers or residents disappearing in the hills behind here."

"Then why does he make the maze? I mean, why bother?"

"Likely, it's in his nature."

"So he just... patrols his own labyrinth, waiting on the off-chance that a hiker blunders down an old gold mine?"

"That, and he's a shifter. For all we know, he goes down there to let off a little steam."

"I feel sorry for him, in a way. All alone down there, wandering his tunnels."

"And likely building new ones. And feeding on any animal who happens into them."

"Still, seems lonely."

"Probably is. Then again, maybe the creature—and the man—are loners by choice. The minotaur could be the perfect expression for the man and the dark master who possessed him."

"Yeah, maybe."

"What are you going to tell your young

client?"

"I have been thinking about that. I think I will convince him that what he saw in the woods that day really was the devil, and that he should stay far away from it. Far, far away from it. And, of course, never talk about it again."

"Isn't that a little... dark?"

"He already believes it's something monstrous. The last thing he needs is to go looking for answers himself."

"But... the devil?"

"Should sufficiently scare him away."

Kingsley shrugs. "Your call."

"So, we're just going to pretend that a minotaur doesn't live in your backyard?"

"Hardly my backyard, Sam. There's a whole canyon back there. He does a pretty good job of keeping a low profile."

"Easy to stay low when you're underground."

"I guess if people really do start disappearing around here, we can discuss evicting him. For now, I say we let it go."

"Okay," I say. "I'll follow your lead."

"How did I go from snuggling with you on the patio to fighting off a minotaur?"

"Because I'm not your average gal?"

He chuckles. "No, Sam Moon. No, you are not."

We are silent, even if the night is not. Crickets and frogs pulse and chirp and croak. I look at Kingsley. He looks at me. I know that look. I like that look.

"So, umm..." I begin, "should we pick up where we left off?"

"Snuggling on the patio?"

"Unless you have a better plan..."

"Oh, I have a few ideas."

"Really? Do tell."

He grins. "Better I show you."

And with that, I find myself in his arms, moving swiftly through the house and up the stairs... all the way to his bedroom with its massive, king-sized bed... built special for my massive, king-sized man.

The End

~~~~~

The thrills continues in:
Moon Tales
Eight Vampire For Hire Stories
by J.R. Rain
Available now!

~~~~~

If you enjoyed this collection, please help me spread the word by leaving a review. Thank you!

MOON SHOTS

About J.R. Rain:

J.R. Rain is the international bestselling author of over seventy novels, including his popular Samantha Moon and Jim Knighthorse series. His books are published in five languages in twelve countries, and he has sold more than 3 million copies worldwide.

Please find him at: www.jrrain.com.

Made in United States
Troutdale, OR
05/19/2024

19969216R00159